BLUE SKY

Brian Kindall

A gift for Jessica Park
from Mr. Zownir

Blue Sky

PART ONE

CHAPTER ONE

OLD STONE WAS THE only one who saw what happened that day. He was up on his favorite ledge, dozing. He liked being there by himself, away from the rest of the herd. He liked how the early morning sunshine felt on his fur. It warmed his aching bones; it soothed his broken horn. But mostly he liked watching the sparkling white glacier bending away down the steep canyon. When he listened closely, he could hear the ice moaning deep down inside of itself. That sound was the closest thing to music that the beast had ever known - the lulling, motherly voice of the mountains.

Old Stone was enjoying all of these little pleasures when he spied the tiny figure coming up the moraine.

"Hrumph!" he grumbled. "What a nuisance."

Of course, it was not so unusual to see humans in the massif. Over the years, the old buck had seen his share. But he had never seen one moving so swiftly, with such confidence and skill. And to his recollection, he had never seen a man alone.

In spite of the annoyance, Old Stone found himself curious. He watched the lone hiker travel through the boulder field, and then scramble over the snowy bergschrund to the base of the tallest spire.

The old ibex chuckled to himself.

Although many had tried, no human had ever climbed to the top of that looming needle of granite. They always had to back off. *Always*. It amused Old Stone that here was yet another person to give it a try.

But then the man made a gesture that caused Old Stone to take notice. Gently, almost like a prayer, he placed both hands, palms flat, against the rock. And then he bowed his head.

Old Stone leaned forward, unsure of what he was seeing. It seemed that maybe - Could it be possible? - the man was listening to the voice of the mountains. He was hearing the music. Old Stone had never thought humans capable of anything but silliness. They were always yodeling and hopping around on the rocks like a bunch of clumsy, two-legged rabbits. They certainly didn't seem to belong in the high mountains. But this fellow here, he was different somehow. Old Stone felt that it was true. This solitary man seemed to be a natural part of the alpine world. He seemed akin to the noble ibex.

Old Stone couldn't help himself; he suddenly liked this man.

Tipping his face to the sky, the man peered all the long way to the top of the spire. He reached up and curled his fingers around a knob of stone. He jammed his boot toe into a crack. And then, with a mighty upward heave, he began to climb.

Up and up he moved, a tiny soul scaling that immense granite wall toward the blue heavens.

Old Stone never took his eyes off the man all afternoon.

The sun crept overhead, raking over the peaks and

casting shadows across the glacier. The air grew cold.

And still, the man climbed upward, tirelessly upward.

After many hours, the ibex thought to himself, My goodness! He's going to make it!

Old Stone was surprised to find himself growing nervous for the man, as if he cared one wit for what humans did with their lives. He thought, I'm going to see the first person climb it all the way to the top.

But then the man stopped. Something had blocked his way.

Stiffly, Old Stone stood, squinting across the chill space.

The alpinist had reached the most difficult part of the route - an overhanging roof of stone. He leaned out from the rock, reaching up and feeling for something secure to hold onto. Then he pressed back tight against the wall, hanging on with one hand, while opening and closing his other hand into a fist.

"Come on," whispered the ibex. "You can do it."

After a short rest, the climber leaned out again, his back arched, an arm stretching out to clutch at the rock above his head. He took hold with one hand - two hands - and then, delicately, he let his boots come away from the wall.

Old Stone gulped.

The man hung with nothing but the yawning space of air between himself and the boulders far below. He swung back and forth, back and forth, like a rag blowing in a light breeze.

For a time, everything stopped.

Even the music.

The whole world held its breath.

"Come on, Friend," whispered Old Stone. "Find your way."

The man seemed to be thinking. He appeared to be considering all the choices before him.

"Find your way." The old ibex was almost pleading. "Please find your way."

The man laughed once - Ha! - and then said something in a language Old Stone didn't know.

His small, human voice echoed in the vast wilderness.

It caused the hairs to rise on Old Stone's neck.

The alpinist held on for a while longer.

But then he did the most horrible thing imaginable.

He fell.

CHAPTER TWO

AS THE ALPINIST FELL, so, too, did Old Stone's heart plummet away inside of him.

It dropped both slowly and quickly at once - like a feather; like a rock.

The man's body scudded along the cliff - down and down and down - turning gruesome cartwheels in the air, as if he were some stone angel toppled from the steeple of a very tall church.

And then he struck the bergschrund.

The sound of it made Old Stone wince.

The man's limp form bounced once, slid for a ways, and then came to rest on the crusty snow.

The air was still.

For a while, Old Stone couldn't make himself move. He stood transfixed by the awful spectacle of what he had just witnessed. But even more than that, he was held frozen in place by a memory that the climber's tumble had awakened inside of him.

"Oh," he said aloud.

Before Old Stone was old, so long ago, when he was still in his very first year on earth, he had watched his own mother fall to her death. Until this moment, Old Stone had managed to hide the memory of that terrible day in his deepest thoughts. But now he breathed a sad sigh that seemed as if it had been waiting inside of him for all of his life. His honey-gold eyes blurred with tears. He shook his great horny head.

"I should just go," he told himself. "The human world is theirs, and ours is ours. They're not meant to touch and cross over."

He stamped a hoof.

"I should climb over the hill and not look back."

But then, from across the canyon, he heard a small groan; the man was not yet dead.

"Oh," said Old Stone. "Oh."

Although their friendship had been a brief one, the fallen alpinist was still his friend, nevertheless. There was no question in the old buck's mind about the right thing to do. Old Stone didn't feel that a dignified being - be he a beast, or otherwise - should let a friend die alone if he could help it. Surely, thought Old Stone, the man would do the same for me.

And so, as quickly as his decrepit legs would carry him, the ancient ibex picked his way over the scree and rubbled ledges to where the man lay dying.

Old Stone had seen some peculiar things in his day. The mountains, after all, are a mysterious world peopled with spirits and whispering legends. But nothing had prepared him for what he found waiting at the foot of the spire.

Panting and limping, he struggled over the last swell of boulders and ice to find not only the man lying like a broken doll, but kneeling at his side - a woman!

Old Stone stopped short. He had never thought of humans as anything special to look at, but he was as shocked by the woman's elegance and beauty as he was by her presence. She was all dark hair long-flowing over clean-white shoulders. She was sad-smiling mouth and knowing-blue eyes. The woman held the man's head in her lap, brushing his cheek with her fingers and singing a happy-sad song.

At first, Old Stone was astonished, then embarrassed. He felt he had stumbled into a private moment where he didn't belong. He didn't know quite what to do, so he just held still, respectfully watching and listening.

Her song, thought Old Stone. It's like the glacier song, only warmer.

He didn't know exactly what he meant by that, how it could be so, only that it was very true.

He thought, Her voice is the voice of the mountains.

The woman held the man close, singing her haunting lullaby, until his last breath left his body. Then she kissed him on the cheek, stood, and faced the old ibex.

Old Stone was too old to be scared by mysterious things, but still, he trembled when the woman stepped toward him. Am I awake, he asked himself, or am I dreaming?

Something told him it was both; he was awake and dreaming at the same time.

The woman's gaze met Old Stone's. It seemed as if she were looking at him from some lost wilderness inside of him. She smiled sadly, bowed her head, and gestured to the side with her open hand.

Old Stone turned to see what she was showing him. The day was ending, the light fading, but he saw something wiggling in the shadows at the edge of the snow, and then, when he realized what it was, his eyes grew large and he looked again.

He turned back to the woman, but she was already gone - vanished into the cold air in that magical way of dreams.

"But..." stammered the ibex. "But I..."

The dead alpinist lay stiff and still where he had fallen.

"But I am an animal," said Old Stone to the lifeless man. "Your world is yours, and ours is..." Before he could finish, the ibex realized it didn't matter. In fact, it wasn't even true. Different worlds *do* meet and cross over. How had he not realized it before? But it didn't make him feel any more comforted. Not at all.

"What a predicament!" The animal snorted in frustration. He stamped at the snow. "I should just walk away," he told himself. "What does it matter? I am old. Surely this can't be expected of me."

But then he heard the creature whimper - that sound that even the hardest heart can't make itself ignore.

"Bother," he said. "And more bother."

Old Stone felt himself drawn to that cry. He felt himself slowly walking over. And then he stopped and looked down.

There on the snow, gazing up at the old ibex, like some lingering shadow of a dream, lay a wiggling human baby. She cooed and sucked at her tiny fist. Her other little hand fell against Old Stone's hoof.

Old Stone felt his heart melt at once.

And in the next moment, he felt a tremendous weight of responsibility settle onto his back like a heap of large boulders.

He didn't know how it had happened. Hadn't he just been enjoying the sunshine and minding his own business? He hadn't asked the man to come into the mountains, hadn't asked to become his friend. But now he was suddenly the godfather to the baby of a man and his beautiful dying dream. "Goodness!" he said. "Heavens!"

The little girl squirmed and fussed on the snow.

Old Stone examined her closely. What a simultaneously odd and beautiful creature she was - so hairless and white.

Then he peered into the sky. The first stars were coming out, cold and blue as eyes watching down on him. He had never seen them in this way before, but now it was so obvious that that was what they were. In some intangible way, they gave him strength.

He sighed. "Okay," he said to the sky. "I will try."

The old beast knelt before the babe and, in that dexterous animal way that an ibex uses its horns like human arms, he gently - oh, so gently - scooped the girl onto his head, holding her in place between his good horn, his broken horn, and his stiff furry ears. He stood, his neck bent slightly forward for balance.

"All right, little one," he said to his burden. "Hold tight. My legs are shaky, and we have a long way to go.

CHAPTER THREE

"CAN YOU HELP?"

It had been a long night. The rasp in Old Stone's voice gave away his weariness.

The doe gazed down at the baby human nestled in the heather at her feet. The little girl's dark wisp of hair lay damp and flattened by the morning dew. She clutched a yellow flower in her tiny fingers.

"Nan?" said Old Stone, when his friend didn't speak.

Without taking her eyes from the child, the bewildered doe answered, "Yes, of course, Stone. You know I will do what I can." She turned her head from side to side, trying to see the child more clearly. "It's just..."

Old Stone sighed. "I know," he said. "The way of the high mountains - the way we've always been taught. Their world is theirs, and ours is ours. But..." he said, and raised his grizzled face to the sun breaking over the ragged skyline. "I've seen some things. I believe it is different from how we thought. I believe it is the right thing to do."

Nan bent over the baby and nuzzled her with her nose. "Yes, of course."

The baby giggled and waved her flower.

"It's just," Nan continued. "Well, don't you think Tor will disagree?"

"I have no doubt. It is his way to disagree with anything I say. But he and the other bucks won't return from the crags until autumn. Perhaps by then we'll understand more clearly where the child belongs."

Nan nodded thoughtfully.

Behind her, at the edge of a small tarn still half covered in ice, the other does and their young ones were having their morning drink, stealing glances over to where Old Stone and Nan were discussing the child. Two curious boy ibex crept over for a closer look.

"Brownie!" called their mother. "Tuff!"

The young bucks laughed and bounded off, kicking up their heels and shaking their hornless heads.

"The others might be harder to convince than I," said Nan.

Old Stone looked toward the tarn. "Yes," he said. "They will have fears. That's understandable. New ways are scary at first. But they are mothers. Surely that will help them accept the baby."

At the mention of motherhood, Nan's face grew sad. Her eyes glistened.

"I'm sorry," said the old ibex. "I heard it from one of the does. An eagle took your newborn. That is hard."

Nan nodded without speaking.

"But maybe the human child can fill the hole your loss has left inside you. Perhaps tending to the little girl will help your heart to heal."

The doe considered her friend's words.

By now the baby had the flower torn to pieces. Pollen and yellow petals covered her face and she was trying hopelessly to wipe them away. Nan bent and nibbled up the flower parts with her soft lips. The little girl laughed. It was a sound that neither the old buck nor the doe had ever heard before. Ibex laugh so differently from humans. But it was such a sweet sound it caused them both to smile.

"I've never been this close to one of them before," said Nan. "They look so fragile and helpless."

"Her father was an alpinist," said Old Stone, "very strong and brave. Her mother was a mysterious dream. Surely that will serve her well."

The baby girl stretched out on the heather, spreading her fingers and toes and yawning a big morning yawn that caused her little body to shiver all over.

"What's that?" It was the young buck Brownie and his brother Tuff. They had snuck over when their mother wasn't watching.

"She's the newest member of the herd," Nan told the boys.

They both leaned close and sniffed at the little girl.

"Someday, she'll be your good friend," said Old Stone. "She just has to grow a bit."

Brownie glanced sideways at Old Stone, not quite sure if the old buck was joking with him. "She's kind of ugly."

Tuff scrunched up his nose. "It looks like a big white salamander."

"Boys!" The boys' mother came over to the little group. "I'm sorry..." she said, but then, when she saw the baby, she said nothing more, only stared in disbelief.

The others came, too - timid, unsure - until all the does and their young had formed a circle around the human baby.

The girl blinked up into the hovering faces.

For a long time, the group just stood there, marveling at the miracle that had dropped into their animal world. It was a lot to take in.

Finally, one of the does asked, "What will you call her?"

Nan peered down lovingly at her adopted child. The little girl met her gaze and grinned.

"Her eyes are not gold like ours," said Nan. "No matter how much she learns the ibex ways, her eyes will always set her apart. It is important for her to have a name that reminds her she is special, to give her strength when she's alone and away from the herd."

The other does bobbed their horns in agreement.

"Her eyes are blue like the sky," said Nan. "The sky,

too, is mysterious. It's where dreams come down to the mountaintops. So," Nan decided, "her name is Blue Sky."

CHAPTER FOUR

SO IN THIS WAY the baby girl was raised as a young ibex - she was nurtured on sunshine, warm milk, and the crisp clean air of the mountains; she was carried from one high pasture to the next in the cradle of Nan's or Old Stone's horns.

The old buck stopped going off by himself to his secluded ledges. Instead, he spent his days on a perch watching over the does and their young. He kept his keen eyes peeled for the threat of eagles, and he scanned the horizons for storms. Old Stone knew storms were coming - in one form or another - and he took it as his duty to be prepared.

Blue Sky thrived. Whether it was because she had the other nimble young ibex as her example, or because she was partly a dream, the little girl grew fast and became a toddler in a very short time. By solstice she was able to amble around in the wildflowers, and by high summer she had learned to hop and skip. Although it made their mother extremely nervous, the girl soon took to playing hide-and-seek among the boulders with Tuff and Brownie.

She squealed when they found her, and jumped onto their backs.

"No fair!" cried Brownie.

She even learned to laugh like an ibex.

In the evenings, as the heavens filled with the glitter of stars, the herd bedded down together in the shelter of the bluffs. It wasn't the ibex way for a full-grown buck to be with the does in the summer nursery, so Old Stone would come to say goodnight before wandering off to find a bed of his own. Blue Sky - they called her Sky for short - always grabbed a handful of his beard and pressed a damp kiss on the end of his nose. It hurt to have his whiskers pulled like that, but Old Stone found he didn't mind it at all.

"Goodnight, Stone," whispered Nan.

Sky yawned and curled up against her ibex mother, nestling in close against the soft fur on her belly.

"Good night, Nan." Stone peered down at the doe and the little girl. They looked like an image from a dream. "Nan?" he said.

"Yes?"

The buck cleared his throat. "Thank you."

The graceful doe smiled in the twilight. "No, Stone," she answered. "Thank *you*."

That first alpine summer passed in a quick succession of pleasant days and restful nights. The does and their little ones learned to accept Sky as one of their own. The snowy peaks towered above like solemn guardians, their great glaring seracs spilling from the heights in the sunshine.

Occasionally, alpinists could be seen in the distance, working their way up an icy arete, or attempting to scale a sheer face of granite. What drew them here? Old Stone often wondered. He personally had no more desire to visit their home in the low valleys than he did to visit the moon. So why did *they* feel the need to come *here?*

For the most part the ibex paid little attention to the humans, and the humans paid even less attention to them. It was hard to see it otherwise - those clumsy, yodeling bipeds were from another world entirely.

CHAPTER FIVE

THEN ONE GRAY AUTUMN day, as ragged clouds tore at the mountaintops, Old Stone saw the approach of what he had been dreading all summer.

He squinted into the rising wind.

He snorted and shook his horns.

There, in a dark brown line moving along the ridge, the mature bucks were marching toward their seasonal reunion with the does. At the head of the procession, half again bigger than the other animals, his broad sweep of horns arching like scythes over his muscular back, strutted the herd's monarch.

Old Stone clenched his teeth. "Tor!"

Soon the does saw the bucks, too, and a ripple of excitement passed through the herd. Brownie and Tuff, who had been playing tag with Sky, bounded off toward the commotion, calling back to their friend.

"Come on, Sky. Let's go see!"

The little girl, her tangle of dark hair hanging over her blue eyes, started at a run behind her playmates.

"Sky!" snapped Nan.

Sky stopped in her tracks and turned toward her stepmother. She had never heard that tone in Nan's voice.

"Come with us," called Tuff, who was bouncing away with his brother.

"Stay close, Sky," said Nan. "We'll catch up to them later."

Sky watched her friends running with the other animals to the tarn. She wanted to chase after them, but she obediently turned and walked back to Nan, burying a hand in the thick fur on the doe's chest.

Nan licked the girl's elbow. "Today you must stay at

my side and be sure to do as Stone and I tell you." The doe forced a smile. "Do you understand?"

Sky nodded.

Old Stone hobbled down from his post and found Nan just as the other does and their young were coming together with the bucks. Sky heard the laughter. It seemed like such a joyous celebration, but neither Nan nor Stone appeared the least bit happy.

"I'll go first," said Stone. His voice was deadly serious. "Wait here."

Nan gazed toward the tarn where the bucks were drinking and talking with the does. "Be careful, Stone. He hates you."

Old Stone lifted his head and swelled his chest, then he went to meet his challenge.

"Old Stone!" said Tor. "What a surprise. I thought by now you'd surely be dead."

The other bucks laughed nervously at their leader's barbed joke.

"Old stones live a very long time, Tor. You should know that." The old ibex tried to laugh. "How was summer at the crags?"

"Fine, old fellow. The forage was good. Pity you'll never see it again."

"No," said Stone. "I suppose I won't."

A gust of cold wind ruffled the water of the tarn, and all the animals leaned into it until it subsided.

"And what about you?" asked Tor. "Did you just arrive, or have you been coddling yourself in the nursery all summer?"

None of the does laughed at the absurd suggestion of a buck spending the summer in the nursery. Instead, at once, they all looked at the ground to avoid Tor's gaze.

The big buck glanced at the herd, reading their gestures and silence. He narrowed his eyes. "What is it?" he demanded. "What do I need to know about your summer?"

"Tor," began Old Stone. "A most extraordinary thing has occurred. A young one..." He cleared his throat. "A..." Old Stone feebly stamped his hoof, trying to shake the words loose in his head, struggling to find a way to say the delicate thing he had to tell Tor.

"What?" said Tor.

But before Stone could answer, the does parted, and Nan strode into the center of the gathering. At her side, wide-eyed and holding onto Nan's fur, was Sky.

For only one split second did Tor find himself flustered by what he saw before him. His nostrils flared and his thick neck jerked back, as if he had nearly stepped on a snake. But then, in the next instant, the massive animal reared onto his back legs and swept his horns through the wind with an authoritative swoosh. He came down hard on his hooves, shaking the earth.

"What," he boomed, "is this?"

Sky hid her face in Nan's side.

The whole herd shuddered.

All but Nan, who remained steadfast before the leader. "It's something very special, Tor. A gift from heaven."

The monarch laughed incredulously, first glancing at the child, and then looking around at the does. "Have you all gone crazy? Have you forgotten the way of the high mountains?" His glance fell on Old Stone. "Has this old bag of bones poisoned your brains with his nonsense?" He stepped toward the old buck.

Old Stone appeared slight and frail before the threatening leader, but with Nan as his example, he tried to stand strong, with dignity.

"What have you been up to, Old crumbling Stone?"

"Tor," said Stone. "It's so much more wonderful than you can imagine." And Old Stone knew that that was exactly what it was as soon as he said it. This proud, powerful leader of the ibex didn't have it in himself to understand the miraculous responsibility that had been given to the herd. Still, Old Stone knew he had to try. "Can we speak alone, Tor? I will explain."

Tor laughed. He glanced at his herd. There was something of a dictator in his approach to leading, but Tor was smart enough to see it in his does' faces - they wanted him to speak with Old Stone. The monarch understood that it would endear him to the does if he listened to their request. He had to at least pretend. Tor laughed once more. "Of course," he said. "Let's you and I have a little chat, Old Stone. You can tell me what's been rattling around in that dusty old head of yours."

The two bucks - one of them large and dark and built of hard muscle, the other small and gray as a shard of weathered granite - walked away from the herd to the far side of the tarn.

Anxiously, Nan and Sky watched after them.

❋

"Tor," said Old Stone. "For the sake of the herd, please hear me out."

"You are no longer their leader, old one. Have you forgotten? I took that away from you long ago."

"Yes," said Old Stone. "Don't I carry this broken horn as my memento from that day? But there are things I can teach you, Tor, important things I have learned that will help you lead."

"I don't believe that a sagging bag of bones with a broken horn can have anything of worth to say to me, but as it might be amusing to hear, I'll listen."

Old Stone could see that the struggle before him was a big one. He had only one chance to convince Tor that Sky belonged with the herd. He chose his words carefully.

"When I led the herd, Tor, I led with strength, like you. Strength is good. It is the ibex way that their leader should be the strongest animal in the herd. You are the strongest, Tor. No one is challenging that, but..." Old Stone proceeded cautiously. "Someday you may find your strength is not enough to save you. You will have to allow something else. You will have to face your new challenge just as I had to face you."

"That was a glorious day," said Tor. "The herd has

been healthier since you were deposed."

"Perhaps," said Stone. "I'm not arguing otherwise. I am only saying that since that day, I have come to understand some things that were hidden from me before. I have seen some things that I was too blind to see."

Tor lifted his face to the clouds and sniffed the air, as if he were distracted, as if he were not listening to anything the old ibex was telling him.

Old Stone sighed in frustration, but he pressed on. "There is a mystery in life, Tor. That is the reason the humans come into the mountains. Our world is where that mystery shows itself to them."

Tor looked at Old Stone with narrowed eyes.

"I'm not sure how it works," continued Stone. "But I know it's true. The line between our world and theirs disappears where the mountains meet the sky. We are all one. Somehow we are all part of the same dream."

Imploringly, Old Stone stepped closer to Tor. "I believe the human child is somehow a messenger from that magical dream. She is a gift from the stars. We must honor this gift, Tor. You must lead with the wisdom of that mystery. Respect it as you lead the herd."

"I see," said Tor. He raised an eyebrow. "A dream."

"Yes. The child is our key to that mystery. I'm sure she's important to us in ways we do not yet see."

The big leader watched across the choppy tarn to where the does and bucks were milling, waiting. Even over the distance, Sky's slight white figure looked out of place among the brown barrel shapes of the others.

"We will go back now," said Tor. "We have talked enough."

By now the wind was blowing with force, warning of an approaching storm. The peaks disappeared behind the lowering clouds.

Tor hopped onto a tall boulder, the blue-black sky pressing down behind him, his herd at attention below. "Winter is coming," he announced. "We must be strong. It is the ibex way."

Most of the animals nodded in agreement, their horns sawing at the blustery air.

Sky huddled up close between her guardians.

"There is no room for weakness," continued Tor. "There is no room for foolishness if we are to survive the snows." He gazed down at Old Stone with mock concern. "It's too bad, but I'm afraid the old one's mind has finally failed."

A low murmur passed through the herd.

Old Stone felt his heart tighten.

"You does have had your fun this summer, but now it must end. There is no place in the ibex world for doddering old fellows and their human children. It is the way of the high mountains. Old Stone and the girl must go."

The old ibex hung his hoary head in defeat. He knew no one would dare to challenge Tor's decision.

"Stone!" whispered Nan.

Sky cowered at her side.

"No," said Old Stone. "Don't make trouble for yourself. Sky and I will go."

"Nan!" called Tor.

Nan lifted her eyes to the leader still perched on his boulder.

"You will stay," he said.

The slim doe hesitated, then, reluctantly, she nudged Sky toward Old Stone. She gazed after the little girl, and then she squared herself, stepping forward. She shook her head. "No, Tor. I won't stay."

Outraged, the huge buck leaped from his boulder and skidded to a halt before her. His burning eyes and raised, sweeping horns said all he needed to say without words.

"I am her mother, Tor, whether you understand that or not. She needs me."

Tor glared at Nan for a moment longer, as though he were deciding how best to run her through with his horns. But then he sensed the other does watching and took a step back. "As you wish," he snorted. "You have no place in the herd anyway if you are as foolish as that." He turned his back on the three outcasts and strode away. "Go!" he commanded.

Old Stone looked at his friend. He understood the sacrifice she was making. Ibex, after all, are herd animals. An ibex without the comfort and protection of the herd and its leader are as good as lost in the wilderness. But, he understood, even more than that, a mother without her child is too tragic to bear.

Old Stone knelt down, and Sky climbed onto his back. He stood, shouldering his blue-eyed burden, shaking a bit in the knees, buffeted by the harsh wind. Then, with Nan at his side, he hurried as best he could away from the tarn and the other animals casting their pitying looks.

Once they were over the crest of the ridge, Tuff and Brownie came running after. Their mother, a stout doe named Sable, was close behind them. "Stone," she called. "Wait!"

The little group talked out of sight of Tor.

"The other does agreed," said Sable. "In the spring, when the bucks return to the crags, if you…" She glanced at the ground. "Well, if you make it through the winter. We would be pleased to have you all come back for the summer."

"Thank you," said Stone. "That means a lot to us."

Nan agreed.

Then Brownie and Tuff watched as their playmate was carried away from them. They skipped once to the side, butted each other in the ribs, and then stood with their heads held low, sadly watching her go.

Sky lifted her hand to wave goodbye, but then she was distracted by the tiny bites of ice she felt against her palm. She gazed at her open hand, and at the gusty air swirling all around her.

"Oh!" she said, a broad smile spreading over her face.

The world was suddenly full of snowflakes.

CHAPTER SIX

BEARS SLEEP UNDERGROUND; DEER descend to the milder valleys; little birds fly away to warmer climes - only the stalwart ibex dares to face winter head on.

In fact, at first glance, the ibex approach to winter appears almost foolhardy. Instead of traveling lower to avoid the deep snows, the ibex, rather absurdly, climbs higher. Of course, it snows even more on the highest peaks, but the ibex have learned that the relentless wind will beat the snow from the rocks, exposing the sparse lichens and moss that provide their meager winter meals. The granite walls, although treacherously slick with ice, are too steep to hold much snow, making it possible for the animals to move along the narrow ledges. It is a severe world of continual spindrift and deadly cold, but with their heavy fur and long-suffering patience, the ibex are perfectly designed for it. Still, it is no place for humans. And certainly no place for a naked little girl.

But Blue Sky was no ordinary child.

Old Stone had known that from the beginning, and yet it didn't stop him from worrying. Not in the least. Even after Sky survived that first stormy night - and the next - and then even the next - the old buck found himself in a state of constant unease. Although it had been simple enough to fool himself during the summer, what with the wildflowers and sunshine making everything so pleasingly pastoral, he was now beginning to wonder if maybe Tor had been right to send him and Sky away from the herd. With her skinny, hairless little body, she seemed so out of place, more dream than real. Perhaps - just maybe - she didn't belong in the ibex world after all. But then, wondered the old buck, where *did* she belong?

Sky herself found more important ways to occupy her time than to worry. She preferred harvesting the icicles that grew along the cliffs. On clear days, she would snap them off and arrange them in rows, poking them into a windblown crust of snow so that the winter sunlight shined through them, casting sparkles of color over the rocks. When it snowed she collected snowflakes. She let them fall into her long black hair and then held them close to her face, comparing one tiny jewel with the next, never tiring of the variety and beauty dropped one by one like gifts from heaven.

But more than anything else, Sky liked to climb. Old Stone had to turn away; he couldn't watch. It made him too nervous. Being an ibex, he could never understand how a human moved, how they worked those gangly arms, how, indeed, they managed to hang on at all without the benefit of ibex hooves.

"For goodness sake, Sky!" said Nan. "Be careful."

Sky laughed, fearlessly launching her lithe body from one slippery ledge to the next, never losing hold, or so much as misplacing a foot. She tossed snowballs off the cliffs, leaning out to watch them fall and fall and fall until - splat! - they exploded in the deep snow far below.

Old Stone shuddered. "She is her father's daughter,"

he said.

"Yes," sighed Nan. "Let's just hope her grip is more sure."

It was a lonely life - a lonely time for Nan and Old Stone, so far from the herd wintering at the other end of the massif. But although Sky caused them great, parental angst, she also made them immensely happy. They found themselves chuckling at her antics. Sky liked to take icicles and make herself a pair of crystalline horns. She held them on top of her head, snorted, and swept them from side to side. "Tor!" she growled.

Old Stone and Nan laughed until their sides ached.

Then at the end of each day, as the white winter sun slipped beyond the far horizon, the odd little family would gather on the cliff beneath an overhanging rock. Sky gave Stone his goodnight kiss. Then she curled up close against her animal mother.

The sky darkened.

The stars came out.

And sometimes, like a sleepy eye watching over them, the moon.

Some nights, when the storms had passed, there was no sound at all except, very far away, and muffled under many layers of snow, the low moan of the glacier. It never seemed to cease. It ground slowly on its course, forever wearing away at the timeless mountains and making its eerie music.

Sky would often join in, softly singing with the glacier as one might sing along with one's mother. Their song was all sadness and joy and a thousand other inexpressible things mixed up together. It caused a feeling to rise in Old Stone that he had never known. It caused him to think of his own mother, of her kind eyes, and of his long life in the mountains.

Eventually, Sky would grow quiet, snuggle down, and fall asleep.

Far in the valley, even beyond the end of the glacier, like the most minuscule stars in the sky, Old Stone sometimes caught a glimpse of the lights of the human world. He had no way of knowing they were the lights in the village of Étoile. He had never even seen a house. In many ways, he realized, he had never been any closer to those tiny lights than he had been to the actual stars in the sky. Still, he knew there were people down there, living their human lives and dreaming their human dreams. Some of them, no doubt, even dreamed of climbing mountains.

Old Stone turned and watched the little girl in the

starlight. Her breath came slow and steady. She smiled, and laughed quietly in her sleep.

PART TWO

CHAPTER SEVEN

"THEY'RE BACK!" CRIED Brownie. "They're back!"

His voice was somewhat deeper than when Sky had last heard it in the fall.

"Yippee!" yelled Tuff.

The two young ibex came bounding up from the frozen tarn as Sky loped down to greet her friends. The trio came together on a patch of dirty snow, stopping abruptly when their eyes met, and becoming suddenly shy. They stared at one another without speaking.

A wren trilled in the heather.

Brownie butted his head against his brother's shoulder.

"You guys are bigger," said Sky.

"Of course," said Brownie. He reared onto his hind legs and pawed the air with his hooves. "We're mighty bucks." Two short spikes had sprouted between his ears.

Sky grinned.

"You don't look like a salamander anymore," said Tuff.

"A little bit." Brownie corrected him.

"Yeah, a little bit."

Sky stepped forward. She hesitated, then she reached out and rubbed each of her playmates on the nose. The bucks went cross-eyed trying to see her hands.

They all laughed.

"Do you want to play tag?" asked Tuff.

Sky nodded.

"Good." He jumped away. "You're it!"

Like an overdue promise, spring had finally arrived.

"The bucks only just left," said Sable. "The winter was hard. An avalanche took the friendly young buck we called Clip."

"There were many bad storms," agreed Old Stone.

The thawing tarn glared like a jewel under the sun. Nan stomped the powder-blue ice at its edge and broke a hole for drinking.

Soon the others came to say hello. Three of the does were new mothers and their wooly little ones watched Sky playing with Tuff and Brownie on the hillside.

"What kind of animal is that?" one asked her mother.

"Welcome," said a doe. "We've missed you."

"Yes," said another. "We've all missed you and the child - Blue Sky."

"Blue Sky." The other does repeated the name in chorus, as if recalling a vague dream from the long winter, as if saying her name aloud might somehow make the mystery more real.

"Thank you," said Nan. "We've missed you, too."

The band of animals turned to where Sky was chasing her friends in circles around the scattered boulders. The first flowers were only just beginning to break through the patches of melting snow, dotting the hillside with sprays of blue and yellow. One could tell by the way she moved that Sky was happy.

In fact, everyone was suddenly very happy.

No one mentioned Tor.

Sky chased Brownie and his brother over the crest of the bluff. Since it was facing north, and did not directly absorb the warmth of the sunshine, the other side of the col still held a lot of snow.

"Watch this!" cried Brownie. He plopped down onto his rear end, his front legs spread stiff and awkwardly apart, and launched himself down the steep, crunchy snowfield. He quickly picked up speed, moving faster and faster until, when he could no longer hold on, he lost control and did one - two - three widely spaced somersaults before coming to a stop where the slope leveled out above a cliff. He lay sprawled and motionless, like he was dead.

Sky and Tuff waited above.

"Is he hurt?" asked Sky.

"Nah," said Tuff. "He's just faking it."

"Wee!" Brownie jumped up and shook the snow out

of his ears. "That was fun!"

Not to be outdone, Tuff followed his sibling's dare, skidding just a ways farther down the hill before he himself lost control and tumbled into a pile of grunts and snowballs and twisted legs.

Then Sky started down, sliding on her bare feet, one bent leg poised ahead of the other. She glided over the bright snow, weaving graceful turns, her thin shadow racing before her, her long dark hair blowing back, until she came to a controlled and perfect stop beside the boys.

"No fair!" said Brownie, disgusted. "You didn't even crash."

Sky's face was flushed with excitement. She reached down and grabbed a lump of snow, plopping it into her mouth and sucking at its coolness.

"Let's do it again," said Tuff. "Only this time we have to go backwards."

"Wait!" said Brownie. "Look!"

Sky and Tuff turned to see.

Far down the valley, on yet another white slope above the glacier, four tiny shapes were slipping quickly over the dazzling spring snow. In the exact instant she saw them, Sky felt her insides twist into a knot.

"Humans!" whispered Tuff.

The three friends crouched above the cliff, watching in silence.

"What are those long things stuck to their feet?" asked Brownie.

"They're flat sticks," said Tuff. "Clip told me about them. They help them to slide better."

Brownie nodded. "They sure go fast."

Tuff glanced at Sky. "They do it like you do."

Sky stiffened. "No they don't," she shot back, although her voice came out weak and unconvincing.

The four humans swooped and dropped down the hillside, calling to one another as they skied. Even from so far away, Sky could hear that their voices were full of joy and excitement. She had never heard that language before, but she was surprised to find she understood it. The human words made her feel good and bad at the same time. She heard them laughing.

"They're like you," said Brownie.

The three friends didn't speak for a minute.

A stony lump was forming in Sky's throat.

Finally, Brownie said, "Maybe they're your real herd."

"They're not!" said Sky. "I'm an ibex!"

"Well," murmured Brownie, "you sure don't look like any ibex I ever saw."

The salt of her sudden tears stung Sky's blue eyes.

"You better tell her you're sorry, Brownie," said Tuff. "Or I'm going to have to kick your butt."

"Oh, don't be dumb. You know I was just kidding."

"Say it anyway," demanded Tuff.

"Ah, for crying out loud." He rolled his eyes. "I'm sorry, Sky."

She wiped her cheeks with her fingers.

"We better get back," said Tuff. "Mom said we shouldn't let the humans see us if we can help it."

Tuff and Brownie started bounding away up the snowfield, then they stopped.

"Are you coming, Sky?"

Sky smiled weakly and waved them on. "Go ahead," she said. "I'm coming."

The two brothers looked at each other. Tuff bumped Brownie with his head. "Dummy!" he said.

"*You* are!"

Then they ran over the hill.

Sky watched the people below her as, one by one, they dipped out of sight behind the rise. Then there was nothing to see but the blue, S-shaped scars marking the snow where they had skied.

"Hooray!" Sky whispered the words she had heard in the language of the humans. They felt sort of awkward, but good, on her lips. She swallowed and tried again. "This is wonderful!"

And although it made her smile and blush to say it, Sky had never felt so mixed up inside.

CHAPTER EIGHT

IN THE DAYS THAT followed, Sky found herself repeating the human words under her breath. She would slip away behind a boulder just to say them aloud where no one else could hear. She whispered them over and over, letting the mysterious sounds form deep inside of her, roll around on her tongue, and then escape from between her lips with a little puff of air. She couldn't help herself. The sensation felt almost magical.

But it was troubling, too. It was like having an embarrassing secret. Sky knew none of the others could make those sounds. Certainly not Tuff or Brownie. They wouldn't even understand them. So how could she?

She gazed into the cloudless blue sky.

But the sky, although surely full of secrets, offered no answers that the girl could immediately understand.

"So," she finally decided, "I'll go ask Stone."

"Hooray." Sky said the word timidly at first, making barely more than a lumpy sort of rasping sound. Then she tried again, more boldly. "Hooray!"

The old ibex rested with his legs folded beneath him. He smiled reassuringly. "Go on," he urged.

Sky clenched her fists at her sides and cleared her throat. "This is wonderful!"

She said it in the way she had heard the skiers saying it. The phrase sounded like glad music in her head. "Wonderful."

Stone nodded thoughtfully. "I remember that human word," he said. "I heard your father say it right before..." Stone shook his horns and looked past Sky to where the does and their young were grazing below some cliffs on a patch of green. A thin waterfall spilled down the rocks above them, its mist blowing sideways and making a rainbow in the sunlight.

"What does that word mean?" he asked.

Sky translated the human word - Wonderful - into ibex so Stone could understand.

"Interesting," he said.

Sky dropped onto a flat rock next to the old buck. She hugged her legs to her chest and rested her chin on her knees. Her dark hair fell over her thin shoulders. "I know I'm not like the others," she said. "You told me the story of my real parents. I know Nan's not my real mom." She sighed. "I'm not really an ibex."

"No," said Old Stone. "You are not."

Sky shrugged. "Who cares?" She pointed at the animals munching busily on the mountainside. "It seems like all ibex do is eat anyway. It's boring. Eat, eat, and eat. All day long." She turned to Stone. "Well, except for you."

"I've lost my taste for food. The others only have summer to fatten themselves for winter, but a bite of grass goes a long way for an old fellow like me."

"But I don't have to eat at all if I don't want to. And I

think grass tastes disgusting. Yuck!" She made a sour face. "I like water okay, but I sure don't have to have it all the time like Tuff and Brownie. They're always stopping our games for a drink."

"They like to play with you," said Stone. "But they also want to be big strong bucks someday. They need to eat and drink."

"Do humans eat?"

"I'm sure they must."

Sky looked at her hands. "Then I must not be human either."

"Well," said Stone, "I think maybe you're something in between."

"Between what?"

Stone considered. "Well, between worlds."

Sky stared at Old Stone, waiting for him to explain.

The animal shifted uncomfortably on his bed of rocks. He scratched at his bony flank with the tip of his good horn. "Everyone," he began, "has to decide where they belong at some point. For some it's easy. Tuff and his brother know they'll someday go with the bucks to the summer crags. That is their place in the ibex scheme of things. For others, it's more complicated."

Sky turned so that she was facing the old sage, her

back to the grazing herd.

"I don't completely understand why the humans come into the mountains," said Stone. "I would say they don't belong here. They seem out of place to me. I've been told that the air of their world is too thick for an ibex to breathe. We'd suffocate if we went down to their valley. And there are rumors of threatening beasts that might do us harm. But the humans survive here, so maybe none of that's true. Maybe humans do belong here. At least for short visits."

Sky stared at Old Stone as he spoke. She watched her reflection bulging in the mirrors of his golden eyes.

"Their world is a dream for us, just as our world seems to be some kind of a dream for them. How much do we belong in that dream? I don't really know. I seem to want to spend more and more of my time in my dreams. I suppose it's a pleasant distraction from my old age."

The old ibex let his eyes close for a moment. Then, with a smile, he opened them once again.

"But you," he said. "You are very special. I'm afraid you might have to make the biggest decision of us all. The universe is obviously quite huge. Much grander than on old animal like me can ever know. It's a big dream all of its own. But where is your place within it?"

"It's with you and Nan, isn't it?"

"Maybe." The old buck smiled. "But maybe not. You know, Nan and I won't always be here for you. You might have to fend for yourself someday."

"Where are you going?"

Old Stone chuckled. "Nowhere, child. At least not this afternoon. Today I suggest you enjoy the sunshine. You're young. You should be having fun. As for those other things, be patient. I'm sure that when the time is right, you'll surely find your way."

CHAPTER NINE

SKY FROLICKED WITH TUFF and Brownie through the long summer days. She romped. She swam and splashed in the icy tarns. She sat on the rocks and joked with her playmates while twisting her long black hair into a braid. Sometimes she wove chains of yellow flowers and hung them as garlands around the necks of the grateful does. (Even ibex mothers like to look nice.) And although Sky did have fun, and was generally a very happy girl, and well-appreciated by the others, when the herd went off to graze, she often found herself with nothing much to do.

It was during those times that - like one of the eagles circling high in the blue sky - her troubling thoughts came swooping down on her, worrying away at her otherwise peaceful life.

She wanted to be patient, just as Stone had told her to be, but Sky found she wasn't a naturally patient creature. She was not. She kept thinking of how Tor had sent her and Nan and Stone away from the herd, all because she wasn't an ibex. It made her feel restless and guilty. It made her feel bad for her guardians. Sky didn't want them to suffer on her account. Still, as any young girl would, she most desperately wanted somewhere to belong.

And then she thought of the humans.

Their joyful words echoed loudly in her memory. "Hooray," she secretly whispered. "Hooray!"

"Could I do that?" Sky often asked herself, remembering how they had skied. "I look like them, so could they..." She trembled. "Could they be my real herd?"

The idea both thrilled and terrified her.

It caused her heart to pound and her head to ache.

So, to distract herself, Sky started to explore.

In many ways, the massif was like an enormous castle, complete with granite towers and turrets and fortified walls. It went on for miles and miles in every direction, surrounded on all sides by steep valleys gushing with powder-blue rivers. Within the boundaries of that natural moat lay the ibex kingdom. And although she was too innocent to realize, Sky was most certainly that kingdom's princess.

She knew better than to venture toward the crags. That would only cause trouble. Tor and the other bucks occupied that territory, and were not to be disturbed. So, instead, she headed off in the opposite direction.

Mountains and glaciers and glaciers and mountains. That's pretty much all there was to see. But Sky found that each feature of the earth had its own personality. She began to think of one broad spire as male, as if it were a handsome buck. And in the next drainage, she found a group of lovely peaks, all of them gathered around a sun-cupped snowfield like slumbering does.

The glaciers, with their deep and murmuring songs, were always female.

Somehow, although it was in a quiet way, these mountains and glaciers became Sky's new group of friends. True, they couldn't talk or laugh like Brownie and Tuff. They couldn't play tag. But in certain ways, they *did* seem to speak to her as she moved along their shadowed slopes and ledges. Sky felt she knew their language, too, just as she had automatically known the language of the humans, just as she had always felt she understood the subtle language of the friendly stars, and the motherly white moon.

Sky climbed all over the mountains. She breathed deeply of the rarified air. She let the high sunshine fill her up with its energy. Each day was much the same as the last until one afternoon, at the top of a peak where she had never been before, Sky met someone - someone unlike anyone else she knew.

CHAPTER TEN

THE INSTANT SHE SAW her, Sky froze.

She stopped mid-step, mid-breath, indeed, mid-heartbeat.

Sky was just too startled to know what, exactly, she should do next.

There, only three steps from her - with her back turned, and gazing out over the panoramic view of the mountains - stood the elegant slim figure of a woman.

Goodness!

Sky gathered her wits, swallowed once, and then, after quickly deciding not to sneak away, took a cautious step forward.

"Hello." She said it softly at first, barely above a whisper, in ibex. But when the woman didn't respond, Sky said it again, louder this time, in the language of the humans.

"Excuse me," she said, and made a coughing sound. "Hello there."

The woman still didn't turn.

That was when Sky suddenly felt quite silly; that was the instant she realized that the being before her was not made of flesh and blood and breath, but entirely of stone.

"Oh!" said Sky. Relief and disappointment washed through her at once. "Oh, I see."

Sky moved closer to the woman and stood before her. "Well," she shrugged apologetically. "Hello anyway."

The woman was as tall as a grown up person. Even though Sky had never seen one up close, she knew that it was so. Her long hair fell over her clean white shoulders and she held her arms partly spread, her hands open and low, as if she were waiting for a child to run into her embrace.

Sky couldn't help herself; a force overcame her; she laid her fingers on the woman's open palm. It was surprisingly, pleasingly, reassuringly warm.

"I'm Sky," she said, her voice suddenly hoarse.

But Sky was sure the woman already knew her name anyway, and everything else about her for that matter. And what's more, Sky somehow, although only vaguely - in that way one sometimes catches a glimpse of a bright star between thick drifting clouds - recognized the woman as well.

"Maybe," Sky whispered, "from a dream?"

The woman, although motionless and silent, seemed to say yes.

Sky peered into the woman's oddly familiar face. It was pale - not like bright snow, but white like bone, or the moon. She was not formed from the salt and pepper granite of the massif, but from a purer stone from far away. Her smile was so full of kindness and love and it was mixed up with all the happiness and sadness of the whole world. It caused Sky to feel funny around her heart. It caused a profound peace to settle over her, like the calm of a summer morning, or the quiet time after rain.

That good feeling flooded in a wash of sunshine all

through Sky's soul. Happy tears welled in her blue eyes.

"Oh," she said.

And then, overcome once more, Sky was unable to help herself - she leaned between the woman's open arms, closed her eyes, and wrapped her own slim arms around the woman's middle, giving her a big hug.

So many questions stormed through Sky's busy mind.

All through the day she sat next to the woman and mulled them over, one after the next and the next.

"How did you get here?" Sky asked. Although she was pretty sure the humans were somehow involved. But what would inspire a person to shape a woman out of stone and then lug her all the way to the top of a mountain?

Sky shook her head. She felt she was being granted a little window into the mysterious ways of people. Such fascinating creatures!

A plastic rose had been left on the rocks at the woman's feet - a gift, Sky decided, from some alpinist to the lady. Sky turned the faded flower over in her fingers, examining it, sniffing at its odorless pink petals. It was definitely from another world, not at all like the fragrant flowers that bloomed above the tarn.

"What must that world be like?"

Sky had never considered that question so completely as she did now. She tried to imagine it, but she could not. Having never been anywhere but the high mountains, she simply could not fathom the mysterious world of the humans.

Across the steep canyon before her, Sky watched the evening pass over the face of a tall spire. It was by far the most impressive peak in the entire massif, and Sky soon decided that it was male, not so much like a buck ibex, certainly not like Tor, or even Old Stone, but, rather, male like a human, like a strong and kind hearted man.

She turned and looked up at the woman. "Oh, I understand," said Sky, and she bobbed her head. "You've been put here so you can watch that mountain."

Sky turned back to the peak, wondering why. There was some purpose in it, but Sky, being naive in the ways of humans, couldn't quite grasp what it might be. Still, she was sure it was true.

The evening slipped into the front edge of night.

Sky watched with the woman across the distance at the majestic rock tower. It seemed to reach like a hand for the starry heavens. The creeping glacier below made its happy-sad music.

Sky joined in the song.

She sang for the woman.

She sang for the whole world, even the parts of it she didn't know.

She sang because she was suffering an odd and disturbing sort of happiness. But mostly she sang because it was the only way she could find to set free the whelming mystery inside of her.

Of course, Sky had no way of knowing that her song was drifting so far away from her, carried on the breeze to the would-be alpinists in the village of Étoile. Her simple tune tugged at their hearts as they slept. Being innocent and young, Sky had no way of knowing her magical power anymore than she understood that her father's own bones were being pulled into the frigid throat of the very glacier with which she sang.

PART THREE

CHAPTER ELEVEN

ANOTHER WINTER GRIPPED THE massif, this one even more angry and bitter than the last. The lashing snows would not cease. Day after wretched day, and night after miserable night, Nan and Sky and Stone cowered on the exposed, wind-worried cliffs. It seemed the malevolent tempest hoped to erase the mismatched trio from the very face of the earth.

Old Stone grew older by the day. He trembled constantly.

Sky wrapped her arms around his neck.

"I'm fine," he assured her, although it was obvious the ancient buck was teetering precariously close to the edge of his life.

But it was the pitiful spectacle of Nan that caused Sky the most distress.

The doe often lay motionless for hours on end, her legs drawn beneath her, her head bowed, her golden eyes closed tight to the prying wind. Ice rimed her horns and nut-brown fur so that she appeared to meld with the frozen rocks.

Nan and Old Stone went for days without eating. There simply was no food to be had. The lichens and mosses had all become encrusted in that impenetrable glaze of ice that the alpinists call *verglas*.

The ibex both grew specter thin.

They chewed with nothing in their mouths.

Sometimes, Sky had to turn away. Seeing her guardians in such desperate circumstances was just too much for her to bear.

It's my fault, she told herself. They wouldn't be so cold and lonely if they could be with the herd where they belong.

But Sky felt helpless to do anything for them. Singing was no use. The wind howled louder than her loudest, most comforting song. And it was certainly no time for Tor jokes. So she just stared into the oppressive white air, watching the monotony of swirling snow. Every snowflake seemed the same.

If we could only catch sight of a star, she decided, or a sliver of blue sky.

But the wind only laughed at her feeble request.

The storm raged harder.

Sky often thought of the stone woman. She had become a regular visitor to the girl's restless dreams. In the depths of her foggy, half-sleep, Sky and the woman sang together while climbing along the tops of the mountains. They braided one another's hair. They had long conversations, usually about nothing in particular, but sometimes touching on issues that seemed to matter.

Someday I might go explore the world, said Sky.

The woman smiled. *The world is a mote of dust suspended in a singular blue eye,* she said. *There is much for a young girl to see.*

But I want to find my place in it, said Sky. She turned and looked into the woman's moon-white face. *I want to find where I belong.*

The woman put her arms around Sky and kissed her on top of the head. *You will find you belong,* she said, *exactly where you belong.*

Of course, the woman wasn't speaking in ibex, or even human, but, rather, in that nonsensical language of dreams. Sky found that if she listened closely - if she thought about the woman's words in a loose and rolling way - something inside of her, some mysterious secret hidden away in her soul - was able to understand just what the woman was saying.

It always made Sky happy, albeit slightly anxious.

As the winter persisted, Sky spent more and more time escaping to her pleasant dreams. The harsh winds could not touch her there; the darkness was pushed out by the flowers and sunshine. Sky especially liked watching her own reflection in the woman's eyes. They were so familiar and kind.

But then one day, Sky was surprised to find she was no longer dreaming. She was shocked to realize that the clouds had truly melted away, the air was still as glass, and that she was not gazing into the stone woman's eyes, but into a radiant blue sky.

CHAPTER TWELVE

THE STORM HAD FINALLY blown itself out.

The winter slipped into a mild lull.

And like a bird set free from its cage, Sky stretched her arms like wings. She reached for the sun and wiggled her fingers. She took a big breath of air. She even did a funny little dance. Then she turned and, with hands on hips, she scanned the cliff behind the ledge where she had for so long been held captive. "I'm going to explore," she announced.

Nan and Stone looked up from where they were scratching with their hooves at the sun-softened ice.

Old Stone swallowed a frosty morsel of lichen. "Just be careful," he said. "This warm weather is liable to cause avalanches."

"All right."

Nan appeared thoughtful. "Sky," she said.

"Yes?"

Nan glanced at Stone. The old buck, sensing that he was intruding on a mother-daughter moment, limped down to a lower ledge and busied himself by searching for food.

Sky stepped before Nan and ran her finger along the curve of the doe's horn.

"I just want you to always be sure," said Nan. "It wasn't your fault."

Sky tried to smile. "What do you mean?"

"I want you to know that I don't regret a thing. You have always been the greatest gift a mother could have, the most wonderful daughter." The doe nuzzled Sky. "We're not often given such a pure view of the magic in this life. I feel fortunate to have been the one who was chosen to be with you."

Sky shrugged. "I feel lucky, too."

Then the girl and the doe stood facing one another for a long and awkward moment.

Nan's golden eyes shined wet with tears.

Sky knew something wasn't quite right, but she couldn't imagine what it could be. After so much bleak winter, she preferred to think of things more cheerful. She wanted to run free on the mountaintops. She longed to feel her hair blowing behind her. It seemed to her that Nan was being awfully morose for such a gorgeous day.

Sky kissed Nan on the nose. "Don't worry," she said. "I'll be back."

The doe nodded.

Sky turned and started up the cliff, springing over the steep, slabby rocks.

"Sky!" called Nan.

Sky sighed and looked back over her shoulder.

The hungry doe stood on the ledge, the great glacier winding behind her like a patient white serpent.

"Goodbye," said Nan.

A chill passed all through Sky right then. She hesitated. Maybe I shouldn't go, she thought. But the day was getting away. The mountains were calling to her. She felt them tugging.

"I'll be back soon," she said. "Do not worry. Enjoy the sunshine."

Once more, Sky turned to the cliff and hurried to climb away. She knew that Nan was still watching her. She could feel the doe's gaze on her back. But Sky didn't turn to see.

She didn't even wave goodbye.

Although later, whenever she found herself watching the stars, Sky would always wish she had.

CHAPTER THIRTEEN

SKY CLIMBED AS FAST as she could up the ice-smattered rocks. It seemed as if she were flying. After so much time holding still on that claustrophobic ledge, it was just so utterly thrilling to move.

"This is wonderful," she laughed. As she flexed and stretched her supple limbs, she felt she truly understood what those human words might mean.

The snow had wind-packed into a hard crust and,

once she reached the top of the cliff, Sky made good time running along the ridgelines. She knew right where she was going. After all, hadn't she been dreaming about it for weeks?

And now that time was finally here.

The sky was blue.

Her name was Blue Sky.

She ran and ran and ran.

"Hooray!"

The stone woman stood at her usual post, holding her same patient pose, waiting with open arms. But now she was up to her waist in the drifted snow. Her hands were buried to her wrists. She looked as if she were wading through swirls of stiff, white water.

At first, it shocked Sky to see her like that.

"Oh, no!"

Somehow, Sky had imagined that when her back was turned - when she was away from this place - the woman was able to move at will, just as she did in Sky's dreams. The woman was at least able to free herself from the snow. But now Sky realized it wasn't quite as she had imagined. The fog between what was real and what was dream was thin, yes, but there was still a small difference between one and the other.

Sky dropped to her knees before the woman of stone. Even kneeling, the hard packed snow held her up so she was able to look directly into the woman's lovely face.

"Hello," said Sky. "I'm back."

Hello, said the woman. *My soul soars to have you near.*

Sky smiled. She brushed the snow from the woman's arm and her cheek. Sky had learned that when she was with the woman she needed to speak the language of dreams.

Would you like me to move away all the snow? asked Sky. *Would you like me to find your flower?*

No. That's not necessary. The rose is resting in my heart. And spring will come to melt the snow.

Sky nodded. She rested her hands on her thighs. *You know, I've dreamed of you.*

Yes, said the woman. *I've enjoyed our times together. Thank you. A dream needs its dreamer as much as a dreamer needs its dream.*

Sky sighed, letting her shoulders slump. *Sure,* she

said, and scratched at the snow with her fingernail. *Still, sometimes I wish you were really here.*

The woman laughed. *That's silly. How am I not really here?*

Sky blushed. *You know what I mean.*

She knew the woman was right - of course, she was here - but she was just as soon not here, too. It was sort of how the mountains were Sky's friends, but they couldn't really play tag like Tuff and Brownie. It was too confusing to explain. Sky didn't really understand it herself. It embarrassed her that she had even said what she did. She turned her back to the woman.

Don't feel bad, said the woman. *Just try to remember - I am no more not here than is my rose under the snow. I am no less here than summer just because it's winter. Surely you know that summer lives between the snowflakes.* The woman's voice was kind. *You must know that I am as present as the stars in the blue sky.*

Sky lifted her face to the scene before her, to the wide blue sky and the white-robed mountains. Far across the canyon, on the shoulder of the great peak Sky had come to think of as a man, the sun had warmed a large cornice to the point of its collapse. It broke free and dumped down the cliffs, fracturing into blocks of ice while trailing a plume of glittering white dust. The air was silent for a time, then, once the sound had carried across the distance, a rumble and roar thundered over the glacier.

Far down the canyon, Sky saw other cornices collapsing under the unseasonable warmth of the day. She watched as the masses of snow snapped free from the ridgelines, tumbling slowly at first, and then starting avalanches that poured like smoke down the fluted mountainsides.

Sky shivered.

Neither she nor the woman spoke.

Then, finally, the woman said, *It takes only one restless snowflake to start an avalanche.*

"Whatever that means," muttered Sky.

She had wanted to talk face to face with the woman about where she belonged in the world. That's what Sky had been hoping to do for so long, away from the nonsense of dreams. But now Sky understood that she might be given an answer she didn't really want to hear. She feared that she, too, was somehow like summer hidden between the snowflakes. That really seemed like no place at all to her. Who would want to belong there?

So she didn't speak.

She only sat and watched the avalanches sweeping down the mountainsides.

They looked like rushing, silent ghosts.

The good feeling Sky had when she was running to visit the woman was slowly being replaced with a sort of melancholy confusion.

Then, as if reading Sky's mind, the woman said, *It will come clear to you. Eventually the clouds roll away to leave us with a blue sky.*

That made Sky feel better.

She turned back to the woman. She held out her hand and laid it on the statue over the woman's heart.

Thank you, said Sky.

Thank you for visiting, the woman answered. *It's good to see Blue Sky in winter.*

Sky smiled.

But now you must go, said the woman. *The mountains are whispering. The old one needs you.*

CHAPTER FOURTEEN

SKY RETURNED TO THE ledge at dusk.

She let herself down from the cliff and turned to find Old Stone standing there hunched and alone, peering toward the shadowed valley far below. He held himself still as a statue, listening to the glacier's plaintive song while watching for the tiny lights of Étoile.

When she saw him, Sky felt something fall inside of her. She was overwhelmed with dizziness. She held her arms out to her sides to steady herself. Then, gathering her wits and courage, she stepped close to the shaggy old buck with the broken horn, resting her hand on his side.

"Stone?"

The haggard beast turned to the girl. "Ah," he said. "You're back." He smiled in the twilight. "You've explored your kingdom."

"Yes," said Sky.

The old buck's voice sounded distant and odd, as though he were almost speaking in the language of dreams, but not quite.

"Good," he said. "Good."

Sky licked her lips. Something wasn't right. She knew it. She had known it the whole time she was running back to the ledge. Even the air on her skin felt wrong.

"Stone...?" Sky couldn't find the words she needed. Old Stone's shining eyes caught her off guard. They made her weak. "Where..." She began again. "Where is Nan?"

"Ah," he said. "Yes. My dear friend Nan." Again, he gazed out over the glacier and dark mountains. "She was resting," he said. "Like my mother when I was young. We used to rest on the clear days in winter. I would curl up next to my mother and the sunshine warmed us." The old buck smiled, remembering those pleasant times. He sighed. "But that was long ago."

Sky shook him with her hand, trying to draw him from his reverie. "But what about Nan?"

"Oh," said Stone. "Yes." He nodded thoughtfully. "It was like a silent eagle. When one is least expecting it. From out of the clear blue sky. The way it took Nan's little one," he said. He paused, tipping his horns toward the abyss, and then he said, "An avalanche carried her away."

At Stone's words, Sky felt as though she had been kicked in the stomach. She doubled over. "Whaaa!" All the wind rushed out of her at once.

For a moment, she couldn't make herself move. She became rigid as stone. Then she dropped to her knees and peered over the ledge, straining to see the bergschrund far below. "Nan," she whispered. "Nan."

Sky whirled around to Stone. "We should go to her!" she cried. "Why are you just standing there? We should go and help her!"

The old buck squinted into the darkening sky. "No," he said. "I was right beside her. I saw everything. It was like it was with my mother. I know. There is no reason to go to her now." He stamped the ledge with his hoof. "She is already gone."

Right then Sky was overcome with a wrenching spasm. It caused her body to heave with sorrow.

"Oh!" she wailed, and wrapped her arms around herself. "Oh, Nan."

At first Sky was too stunned to completely comprehend. It made no sense. How could Nan be there one instant, and then be gone in the next? It was too impossible to imagine, and too horrible.

But then she began to see how it was - the mountains were friends, yes - they were home for the ibex, and a playground for the humans - but they could just as soon become deadly.

Sky had never realized that before; although she had known it in ways, she had never truly known.

But now she did.

It was hard-edged truth cutting into her.

There was much to lose, she now understood, in living so close to dreams.

Sky felt a certain innocence fly away from her that evening.

She felt an emptiness opening up inside of her.

And then the young girl sat on the ledge next to the old ibex. She held her face in her hands, her dark hair falling over like a veil as she wept and wept beneath the ever-watchful stars.

CHAPTER FIFTEEN

SOON AFTER, THE MEAN-HEARTED winter returned with a vengeance.

It was made all the more dreary with the absence of Nan.

The stinging, wind-whipped snow pelted the peaks as Old Stone and Sky lay huddled together on their lonesome ledge. The stars and blue sky disappeared. The sun was extinguished. Spring became a hope to be put away and forgotten as one storm after the next breathed an icy death over the mountains.

During those bleak times, Old Stone sought refuge in his reveries of childhood. Sky could hear him chuckling quietly in his delirium, and she knew he was revisiting the sunny summer pastures of his youth, bouncing again in the wildflowers and pestering his mother for a warm swallow of milk.

The old buck's pleasant dreams stirred Sky's own memories of her happy times with Nan. She remembered the doe's golden eyes and gentle ways. She remembered her courage and kindness. But then those memories always led Sky to feel bad about that last day she was with Nan on the ledge.

I should have been more understanding, thought Sky. I shouldn't have been so restless. Nan knew she was telling me goodbye for the last time, and I was just a silly girl and eager to get away.

That dark day weighed heavily on Sky's heart.

"She did so much for me," whispered Sky.

It's all right, the stone woman assured her in a dream. *She loved you. She loved you as the sunshine loves its flower. She loved you deeply and gratefully and wholly.* The woman laid her hand on Sky's shoulder. *She loved you in ways I was unable to myself.*

By now Sky had come to suspect - if only vaguely - that the stone woman was her true mother, although she had no idea how that could be so. Like so many things in her life, its explanation was hidden behind a fog. She knew, of course, that it had something to do with the mystery of dreams, but being only half a dream herself, it was lost to Sky how it worked. She only knew what she felt, and what she felt was that her mother was somehow the spirit of the woman of stone, and her father was a mystical part of the great peak that the statue had been created to watch over.

It was that and so much more.

It was at once much bigger, like the sky, and very much smaller, like a single flake of snow.

It was a secret dream language whispered upside over and backwards into her ear on a windy day, and it only made Sky's head hurt all the more when she tried to figure it out.

Just know that it's good, the stone woman told her. *Be sure that it's quite lovely and good.*

So that's what Sky tried to do.

"It's good," she told herself, over and over again. "It's good. It's good. It's good."

Although always niggling in her deepest thoughts was the worry that it might not be as good as she hoped, and that it was probably up to her alone to make her life as truly good as she needed it to be.

But how, thought Sky, am I supposed to do that?

CHAPTER SIXTEEN

WHEN SPRING FINALLY DID arrive, it came with far less joy than Sky had hoped it would. The sunshine seemed less sunny than she remembered, the flowers less bright and cheerful. She missed Nan. The doe's death had left a hollowness in the girl that couldn't be filled with anything so commonplace as warmer weather. And then she learned that Old Stone had no intention of rejoining the does at the tarn.

"That was only for when you were small," he told her. "That is not my place. It wouldn't be right, not the ibex way. I'll just stay here." He closed his eyes. "But you should certainly go," he said. "I'm sure the does will be glad to see you."

Sky was hesitant to leave the old animal's side. The long winter had been so hard on him. He was more frail than ever, barely able to walk. She thought to herself, what if he needs me when I'm not here? And what if he should... She could barely stand the thought. What if he should die?

"I'll be fine," said Stone. "Please go. You've been languishing here long enough."

Sky waited for two more days, but then she began thinking of Tuff and Brownie - of playing tag and telling jokes and sliding down the slopes of spring snow. She felt somewhat selfish about it, but that certainly sounded like more fun than sitting with Old Stone while he napped. So, reluctantly, on the morning of the third day, she kissed the old buck on the nose, whispered a goodbye into his ear, and then traveled across the wide massif.

"Hooray!" she shouted under her breath. She said it in human first, then in ibex, then, again, in human. "Hooray! Hooray! Hooray!"

But she felt little of the word's meaning in her soul.

"Blue Sky!" said Sable, with a warm smile. "Welcome!" The doe gazed over the girl's shoulder. "You're alone?"

Sky bit her lip and nodded.

"I see," said the doe. She stepped close to Sky and gently nuzzled her arm. "I'm sorry, dear. It was a hard winter for us all."

Sky scanned the hillside where the other does were gathered on some open ground below a rocky bluff. The animals glanced her way, some of them smiling and lifting their horns in greeting, but none of them came to say hello. They were too busy tending to their young ones and nibbling the succulent shoots of new grass.

One little blond ibex skipped over and stood beneath Sable's belly, staring out at Sky with big eyes from between the doe's front legs.

"This is Pebble," said Sable. "She's my newborn."

Sky knelt on the heather. She bent toward the tiny creature, reaching out with her hand. "Hello there, Pebble."

The little animal leaned forward and sniffed at Sky's

palm, flicking her tongue at the air above the girl's fingers. But then she quickly ducked back and hid her face against her mother's leg.

Sky stood. "Where are Tuff and Brownie?"

"They went with the bucks this summer," said Sable. "To the crags."

"Oh," said Sky. A pang of longing shot all through her. "Well," she said. "Good for them. After all, they want to be mighty bucks, so that's where they belong."

"Yes," laughed Sable. "They are quite determined to grow big and strong. It's funny to see them strutting around, butting their heads and flexing their muscles. They measure their horns every day."

Sky grinned at the thought of the silly boys acting all grown up.

"Are you going to stay with us this summer?" asked Sable.

And as soon as the doe said it, Sky knew that she could not. She shook her head. This, she suddenly realized, is no longer my place.

"No," said Sky. "I'm just visiting. I just wanted to say hello and..." Sky swallowed and tried to smile. "I just..." She shrugged.

"Well," said Sable. "I understand."

Pebble butted her head against her mother's tummy, nagging her to join the others.

"Well," said Sable. "It was good to see you."

"Yes," said Sky. "Please say hello to the boys when you see them."

"I will, dear. You take care of yourself."

"Of course," said Sky. There seemed nothing else to say. "Goodbye."

"Goodbye."

Then Sky turned from Sable and the beautiful tarn, but it seemed as if she were turning her back on so much more. Sky felt as if she were turning her back on her happy childhood. She knew that the does were watching her. Even Pebble was watching her go, slipping away like a dream to be forgotten.

But Sky didn't turn back.

She just kept walking.

She didn't want them to see her tears.

PART FOUR

CHAPTER SEVENTEEN

LONELY AS FOG, SKY drifted into the wilderness heart of the mountains.

This was that stark and stony region beyond the wildflowers, well above the pleasant summer pastures of the ibex.

She traveled across the ice-clad canyons and scaled the severe granite peaks.

She never slept; hadn't she slept enough in winter? And for a while at least, she had had her fill of dreams. She needed a break from their confusion.

Besides, she was too busy looking for something - surely she was - something she had misplaced long ago - although she didn't know just what it was. She only hoped she would recognize it when she found it.

"I just have to keep hold of my faith," she told herself. "I just have to be brave."

She wandered and wandered, always searching, searching.

It was as if she were the sole inhabitant of a very large castle, and with the discovery of each empty chamber - with the exploration of each deep corridor and each tall tower of stone - the girl only found herself feeling ever more vacant and alone.

She struggled with her own despair.

But she pressed on.

Old Stone had once called these mountains her kingdom.

"But what," asked Sky, "is the good in that?"

What was the point of being the princess of such a

barren place? Sure, it held a certain wild beauty. Sky knew there was no place like it. It *was* extraordinary, truly magical in so many ways. But it seemed a world apart from any world that truly mattered. And without someone to share it with - without someone with whom to laugh - Sky felt she just as well be princess of the moon.

The alpine summer crept along - days and nights, lonesome days and lonesome nights.

Sky dove to the bottom of the milk-blue tarns, and then floated with the dwindling ice on the surface.

She absentmindedly braided her long black hair, let it all come down, and then braided it up again.

Sometimes she lay stretched out on a flat rock in the sunshine, gazing into the deep blue sky, and listening closely to the tantalizing song of the glacier. Such a haunting sound.

But Sky didn't sing along.

She did not.

As much as she longed to, Sky could no longer find it in herself to see the mountains and glaciers as her friends. After all, these mean-hearted mountains had taken Nan away from her. And hadn't they taken her father as well?

She once asked the stars, "Is this really where I belong?"

But the stars, so distant and cold, had become sleepy and silent.

Sky felt all the more alone, all the more hopeless, until, one quiet night, from out of the depths of her gloom, she felt a sensation she had never felt before.

She tensed, holding herself perfectly still.

Someone was reaching for her, someone stirring in some hidden place inside of her.

She held her breath.

Her eyes were wide.

And then that someone touched her lightly, taking hold of her with a gentle hand.

"Goodness!" gasped Sky. "Oh!"

CHAPTER EIGHTEEN

SKY KNEW JUST WHAT was happening without knowing how she knew.

Someone was dreaming her - someone who was close to her, but whom she had never met.

"Oh!" she gasped. "Oh!"

It was unsettling, but thrilling, too.

It felt as though the dreamer were nudging her back to life, melting the deep winter snow that had drifted into her melancholy soul.

It made her anxious; it made her happy.

Sky squinted into the black air, straining to see who it was. She could only just make out a light shadow - the thin silhouette of someone earnest and brave, someone young, like herself, and full of high hopes.

Who are you? asked Sky.

I am an explorer, came a voice, *and I am coming to discover you.*

Sky shuddered. The dream was being born from another world, a mysterious people-world full of things and ways Sky didn't understand. She was surprised to find herself so frightened.

When will you come? asked Sky.

I will be there, of course, when I get there.

Sky shook her head. *But how will I know it's you?*

You will know, laughed the shadow, *because you will see that I am the snowflake like none of the others.*

And then, still ringing with laughter, the dream faded away.

Wait, called Sky. *Don't go!* "Come back!"

But it was no good. She felt the dreamer release her, like a hand letting a rose gently slip from its fingers.

Sky drew a big breath of night air, then let it out over her lips, making a hollow whistling. "Sometimes," she said, "I just hate that silly nonsense language of dreams."

She stood on a rock, tipping her face to the heavens.

She stared into the stars, and then into the fathomless black places between those stars.

A single meteor burned a quick bright trail over the mountains, and then vanished.

Sky shivered.

She wrapped her arms around her middle, squeezing herself tight while recalling something the stone woman had once told her.

"It must be true," said Sky.

Smiling in the darkness, she whispered it to the stars.

"'A dream needs its dreamer,'" she said, "'as much as a dreamer needs its dream.'"

CHAPTER NINETEEN

IT FELT ODD TO both need and be needed; it felt scary and joyful and new.

And yet Sky was certain this was the secret thing she had been searching for in all her wanderings around the wild massif. This, somehow, was that treasure she had lost so long ago, even though she had no recollection of ever having it before in her life.

"But what do I do now?" she wondered.

She looked at her hands.

"Do I go and find my dreamer? Or do I wait here?"

Finding that her hands held no answers, she closed them into fists and tried harder to think what to do. She desperately wanted not to make a mistake. She did not dare blunder this opportunity. But never having been in someone's dream before, Sky lacked the skills of a well-practiced, full-fledged dream.

"I'll just hold still," she resolved. But then, after only a single second of holding still, she decided, "No, I will go and find my dreamer."

Sky started off at a run, springing from one starlit boulder to the next. Then she realized she had no idea where she was going so she stopped right where she was.

"Oh!" she said, and glanced in every direction around her - mountains and mountains and more dark brooding mountains, and not a single dreamer in sight.

"No," she said. "I'll wait."

She forced herself to sit down. "Yes." She crossed her arms over her chest. "That's what I will do - wait."

But Sky, being a naturally impatient creature, could not wait.

"Argh!" she cried, and jumped up once again. She stamped her foot. "This is ridiculous!"

With her hands on her hips, she said, "I need to talk to someone who knows how this whole dreamer business works."

She gave her head one quick nod.

And then she galloped up the steep rocky slope.

CHAPTER TWENTY

SKY HELD THE PINK plastic rose in her lap, thoughtfully twirling its stem between her fingers while gazing at the impressive manly peak across the way.

What is the difference, she asked, *between a dream and what's real?*

The stone woman - her mother - stood motionless behind her. *One,* she answered, *is only the face of the other. One is the other's echo and shadow.*

Sky rolled her eyes. "Urgh!" she groaned under her breath. Dream talk! She knew it was going to take some effort to understand just what her mother was telling her.

But how do they meet? Sky laid the rose on a rock. *How do they ever come together and touch?*

They are never not touching, said the woman.

Meaning what?

Meaning a finger cannot help but touch itself.

Even though her mother didn't move, Sky sensed that she was smiling in that kindly, know-everything way of grown-ups. It annoyed her.

"That," sighed Sky, "is the dumbest thing I have ever heard."

Sky didn't speak for a moment. She was trying to decide if this conversation was even worth the effort. She did not need riddles right now. She needed real information, the kind that might actually help her with her problem.

Maybe I would have better luck, Sky told herself, just talking to my finger.

A stout and sudden breeze swept over the summit, shaking Sky so that she had to brace herself against its force. It passed just as quickly as it arrived, and Sky wiped the hair out of her face, plucking a strand from where it had caught in the corner of her mouth.

Wonderful, said the woman.

Sky turned and looked up at her. *What?*

The word - wonderful.

What about it?

It's always the same, said her mother. *It's always wonderful.*

Sky shrugged. *So?*

Wonderful, continued the woman, *is wonderful if it is said in a dream, or on the other side of a dream. It is still wonderful if it's said in starlight or ibex or mountain, even if it's said by a rose under the snow, or whispered on the wind by a man falling through the air. A dream and her dreamer are both wonderful.*

Sky nodded slowly. That made sense, sort of. Sky felt, at least, that it was probably true. But it also seemed like pretty worthless information. Wonderful as it was, she couldn't see how it might help her find her dreamer.

Why can't I have a regular mom, she wondered, like Pebble has Sable?

Sky thought of Nan.

She sighed.

Then Sky stood, turned, and stared into her mother's

bone-white face. She took the woman's hands in her own, lightly squeezing her palms. It always surprised Sky how she could sense a bit of warmth in those hands, as if they were flesh and blood, as if her mother were alive and, at least in part, dwelling on this side of a dream.

Sky licked her lips. *How…*

The wind gusted again, interrupting her, and this time Sky smelled the brewing storm. She gazed down the canyon to the clouds coming up fast and swallowing the mountains and the glacier. Those bruise-black clouds were full of menace and electricity. Sky could taste it in the air.

She turned back to her mother. *How did you meet my father?*

Sky knew for sure her mom was smiling now.

Well, said the woman. *How does one meet the beat of one's heart?*

Sky shook her head in the rising wind. *I don't know,* she said, *that's why I'm here. That's what I'm asking.*

Thunder rolled up the canyon. It echoed and boomed and swept away with the wind.

Close your eyes, said the woman.

What?

Turn the blue sky to black, the day to night. It's

easier to see the stars that way.

Although it seemed silly, Sky did as she was told.

Now, said her mother, *listen.*

And in spite of her skeptical self, Sky *did* listen. What was her choice? She listened as hard as she could. But all she heard was the howling wind. The first drops of sleet were blowing over the summit now, and the tiny splats of cold dappled her skin.

Listen to your heart, said her mother.

Okay, thought Sky, and she tried to listen even harder. She thought she might just be able to hear the glacier music, even over the storm, but she could not hear her heart. Try as she might, she simply could not. She tipped her head to the side. She leaned into the pushy wind.

It's no use, she shouted.

Listen, her mother said calmly, *with that part of yourself that knows how to hear.*

And just as those words took hold in her thoughts, something inside of Sky understood exactly what her mother was telling her.

"Ah," said Sky, and she listened with that part of herself that was a dream.

All at once, the wind seemed to cease.

Sky felt as if she were surrounded in silence, floating like a star in space.

From out of the depths of that silence, Sky heard, very softly, the ka-thump...ka-thump...ka-thump of her own beating heart. "Oh," she whispered. It felt so soothing. But even more than that, and even more reassuring, Sky felt the rhythm of another heart gently keeping time with her own. It caused her to tremble with unexpected joy.

She opened her eyes.

Once again, the world was full of windy noise.

The stone woman's wet face lit up with a flash of lightning.

Thunder cracked.

Sky gazed at her mother's face for only an instant, noting how her eyes turned blue with the lightning. But then, because it was what her heart was telling her to do, she spun around.

She peered across the swirling space. She bent forward, straining to see. There! Part way up the stone tower. A person was clinging to the rocks!

Then the clouds surged across the canyon, blocking Sky's view.

Just as soon as it appeared, the tiny figure disappeared.

CHAPTER TWENTY-ONE

INSTANTLY, THE CLIFFS BECAME deadly slick, glazed in a fatal mixture of rain and sleet. Even for a climber as gifted as Sky, it was a treacherous place to be. As she picked her way down her mother's peak, she understood how important it was to take care with her every move; she needed to be quite certain of every hold to which she trusted her weight.

And at the same time, she most desperately needed

to hurry!

Thunder shook the air; it shook the earth.

Jagged bolts of lightning sliced down into the canyon, blinding Sky for seconds at a time, and leaving the wind full of the acrid scent of burnt ozone.

When Sky finally stepped off the mountain, she wasted no time. She turned to race across the boulder field. In her eagerness, she slipped almost at once and pitched headlong into the rocks.

"Ah!" she cried. "Ouch!"

Sky rolled onto her back, squeezing her eyes shut tight against the rain, gathering her bearings. But she knew she did not have time for such indulgence. So she jumped right up, shook her hands at her sides, limped a few steps, and then resumed leaping along the edge of the glacier to where it met the sloping bergschrund. Scrambling over that last band of snow, she finally reached the foot of the tallest and most daunting peak in the entire massif.

Sky whipped the wet hair from her face and leaned with her palms pressed against the cold stone, squinting up into the rain while straining to find some hint, some small glimpse, of the luckless climber she had spied from across the way.

"Where are you?" she asked.

There was no answer besides the rush of wind and the noise of falling water. She could see nothing beyond where the glistening gray wall faded into the fog.

Waterfalls dumped from the mountaintop and splashed down the cliff in torrents.

Rocks dropped out of the rolling clouds, thudding like bodies into the soggy snow all around her.

Sky drew a deep breath, trying to calm her panic.

Even on sunny days, this mountain had always appeared un-climbable, more an object to admire from afar than something to approach with any hope of ever reaching the blue sky at its summit. But now, more than ever, it looked utterly impossible.

How, Sky could not help but wonder, do dreams die?

Nan's face flashed in her mind.

And then - quite obscured, and only for an instant - Sky saw the handsome, weathered face of a man. Sky knew at once it was a vision of her father.

"Oh," said Sky, and caught her breath. "Your eyes are not blue." It surprised her to realize. "They're golden," she whispered, "like the eyes of an ibex."

Suddenly, that single fact changed everything for Sky. Somehow, sensing that she was not alone, seeing that she was part of a family - a big family made up of alpinists and dreams and ibex - Sky felt a lift in her courage.

"Wonderful," she said, although she didn't really know why. *Wonderful,* she said again, this time in the language of dreams.

She reached her arm above her head and jammed her fist into a crack, twisting it sideways so that it locked solidly into place. She stepped high, curling her toes over a nubbin of rock. And then, with every ounce of her strength, Sky began climbing like she had never climbed before.

Up.

Up.

Up.

There really are only two directions in the high mountains.

(Sky did not dare consider that dreadful direction of Down.)

The storm had not stopped, but it settled heavily over the range, dousing the mountains with its violent deluge.

Sky crept upward, ever upward, slow as a torpid spider. Each inch gained was a labor taxing her patience and boldness and skill. The slushy rain ran down her arms and over her back. It flowed down the face of the mountain.

"One move at a time."

Sky talked to herself as she climbed. "And then the next.

"And the next.

"And...oops! Careful, Sky. There now. Take hold of that edge."

Sky became so focused on her task that she almost forgot its purpose. But then, out of nowhere, dangling right before her face, she found herself staring at the end of a thin red rope.

It caused her to pause.

It seemed so out of place, more like the idea of a rope than a thing one could actually hold in one's hand.

Sky touched it lightly, running her finger along its braided weave. She grasped it in her fist, squeezing it tight. It made her think of plastic roses. Then, slowly, she let her gaze follow its snaking, twisted path, up the rocks. The red rope was so vivid and otherworldly against the gray granite. She followed its length to where it spilled in loose coils from over a thin ledge.

And there she saw something even more surreal; she saw something that looked so very out of place, definitely some weird image from a dream.

And yet, it was almost beautiful.

Sky found herself smiling at its strangeness.

There, like a tremulous flower blooming from the rocks, curled and dripping with rain, Sky spied a cold, white hand.

CHAPTER TWENTY-TWO

HAD THAT MYSTERIOUS HAND not finally moved - had its finger not twitched in the rain, just once - Sky might have remained frozen in place all day, marveling at it from below while clinging to the storm-racked mountain. But that living, twitching finger managed to shake her from her stupor. It touched that wilderness place hidden in the deepest regions of her soul, causing her to shiver to the core of her bones.

"Ah!" gasped Sky, pressing her free hand to her chest.

In the next instant, lightning pounded the spire. Sky went blind with its hot white flash, and deaf with its explosion of thunder. Heat waves pulsed through the stone beneath her grip.

Then - Whoosh! Whoosh!

Rocks tumbled past in the wind.

Bang! Thunk! Bang! They bounced along the cliff.

Sky hugged the mountain, trying to make herself small.

Once the stone-fall subsided, she immediately resumed climbing, carefully working alongside the red rope, her heart drumming anxiously with the foreboding of what - or rather, of whom! - she might find attached at the other end.

Sky drew close to the hand, and closer still, until she was perched just beneath the dripping ledge. She reached above and took hold of the granite lip. She placed her feet - first one, and then the other - higher up the wall. She flexed her whole body so that it was taut as a spring, and then, with a little grunt of fear and bravery, Sky heaved herself onto the narrow shelf of stone.

Trembling, with rain dumping onto her back, Sky

knelt on the ledge.

At first, she couldn't make herself look at the fallen climber beside her. Much as she wanted to, she could not. Although Sky didn't completely understand the feelings flying around inside her, she knew that so much depended on that person being alive; so much depended on that person being able to look her in the eyes and see that she was really here, and more than just a dream.

Focusing on the rock wall before her, Sky hooked her sopping tangle of hair with her thumbs, tucking it behind her ears. She swallowed the lump of anxiety caught sideways in her throat. She blew a bit of breath from between her teeth. And then, slowly, almost reluctantly, she turned to see who was sharing the ledge with her; she turned to see the first real flesh-and-blood person she had ever met in her life.

He was a boy.

Sky had never seen one before, but she knew that's just what he was. He was like Tuff and Brownie, only human.

He lay on his back up close to the wall, the rain

falling into his freckled face. His eyes were shut. His clothes smelled scorched with lightning. A purple lump, with a small scrape at its center, swelled on his temple in front of his ear.

A happy tremor passed through Sky when she looked at him - he was extraordinary.

But in the next moment, she sensed Death circling in the clouds.

"No," she said, and shook her head. She leaned over the boy. "No," she said to Death. "No."

She reached out and held the boy's hand - icy and wet. For a second she feared he had already left this world behind. But then, very quietly, the boy moaned. He squeezed her fingers.

"Yes!" said Sky. "I'm here. It's going to be all right."

But honestly, when she considered the circumstances, she did not know how to make that true. After all, they were half way up the most severe mountain she had ever known, in the midst of the wildest storm. And now, just to add to their problems, the rain had decidedly turned to snow.

It fell silent and fast all around the pair of hapless climbers.

The boy's clothes were already soaked. He was

dangerously chilled. Sky considered huddling with him on the ledge until the storm passed, but she knew enough about mountain weather to realize it would not pass any time soon. Surely he would be dead by then.

She peered over the ledge. It was such a slippery long way to the bottom. But she felt it was the boy's only hope. She had to get him down.

The red rope was tied around his chest and Sky took it in her hands, examining it. The cord ran a ways up the cliff to where it fed through a metal clip fastened to a crack in the stone. Sky had no experience with climbing equipment. That was something from the people-world. She understood it was somehow used to safely let oneself down from the mountain. But how?

The boy's backpack lay next to him on the ledge, and more of the clips and metal pegs were hanging from short straps. Sky took one of the clips, squeezing it so that its gate opened, and then snapped closed with a click. She bit her lip, trying to put it all together in her mind, trying frantically to understand how the rope and clips worked together as a single tool.

She closed her eyes and reached deeply into herself, reaching for that secret knowledge she hoped was there. She peered into those foggy places where dwelled the skill and wisdom of her alpinist father.

And then, with a rush, Sky saw the answer.

She opened her eyes and smiled.

"Thank you," she whispered.

CHAPTER TWENTY-THREE

SKY WORKED FAST.

She tied the backpack to the extra rope hanging below the boy, so that it was out of the way. Then she pulled up all the slack line and let it dangle in a long loop down the cliff. With the red rope running up through the clip like a pulley - stretching down to both herself on one side, and to the boy on the other - she was ready to go.

Sky peered down the mountain. Snowflakes drifted

thick as feathers through the air. They stuck to her lashes and the rope and the rocks and everything else, too. She couldn't see the bergschrund, but she was certain it was still down there; it was hard and far and waiting to gobble them up if they should make a single mistake.

Sky was not at all confident she was capable of the feat she now imagined herself performing. She knew she was part dream, and that gave her certain benefits of strength not enjoyed by other girls. And she *was*, after all, the daughter of a skilled alpinist. But whether these talents and gifts would work together to her advantage was something Sky had yet to put to a test.

"Well," she said. "There's only one way to find out."

She rubbed her palms together and took hold of the rope.

She gazed again into the sleeping boy's face. "Okay," she said. "Good luck."

And then, without further delay, she placed her feet on his side and shoved him gently from the ledge.

The boy plunged through the snowy air.

The rope jerked tight.

It slipped through Sky's fingers.

Down and down he fell, the wet line buzzing through the clip on the rocks.

"No!" cried Sky, and she clinched the rope tighter. It seared her palms, but she was determined to hold on.

The boy's weight yanked her arms above her head and she was lifted from the ledge.

But then, at once, the falling stopped.

Everything held still.

"Ooh!" groaned Sky. She could feel the boy swinging in space at the end of the creaking rope. She hadn't expected him to be so heavy. The rope slipped a bit more through her fingers, but this time she didn't let go.

Sky gathered her wits, and then - because it was all she could think to do - she slowly twirled her body in the excess rope so that she was twisted in its coils, making herself into an anchor. She let her weight settle into the tangle of rope to take the load. The rope cut uncomfortably into her sides, but now her arms were free and she was able to open her hands and stretch her fingers. Sky looked at the burns on her palms. She held them up in the falling snow to cool them.

"Okay," she said. "Now what?"

She was, after all, in a tricky situation.

But it wasn't long until she saw a way to tie off the end of the rope to a protrusion of stone. She snugged it up good and tight and then let herself unwind from the coils, allowing the rope to gradually feed out through the pulley.

The boy descended a bit farther down the mountain, then stopped.

Sky climbed down to his side.

The boy hung with his chin on his chest, like a puppet in the snow. He didn't move, or even moan.

Sky leaned up close to him to check if he was still breathing. She squeezed his hand and felt, faintly, the quiet thrum of his heart in her fingers.

"Sorry about that ride," she said, and blew her breath into his hands to warm them. "I'll do better next time, I promise."

She fastened the boy to the cliff with clips and straps, climbed up to unfasten the line, and then, again, she carefully climbed back down to his side.

After her first reckless attempt, Sky understood better how to let the boy down the cliff without dropping him so suddenly into space. She wrapped the rope twice around the clip, making it grab with more friction, reducing the load. She also figured out how to allow only half the rope length to pass through the pulley before descending on her end so that she was next to the boy, tying him to the cliff, and then pulling the rope through the clip without having to climb back up to untie her knots.

It was grueling work, and maybe not the way her father would have done it, but Sky and the boy worked their way down the stormy mountain.

Once they reached the bottom, Sky quickly untied him. She was relieved to be off the spire, but it was too soon to celebrate. The air was even chillier now. The snowflakes had grown smaller - more like the snowflakes of winter than those of a freak summer storm - and they were more numerous. Sky knew the cold was creeping into the boy's core, sucking away at the dwindling flame of his life. She had to move faster.

Leaving the red rope hanging on the mountainside, Sky slipped the boy's pack onto her back. She grabbed his coat at the collar and began shuffling, half-bent and backward, dragging him through the snow.

Sky knew right where she was going. It was a special

place she had discovered last winter. On a crisp, clear day, while sitting with her mother on her mountaintop, Sky had spied the telltale puff of steam breathing out of the snow-covered boulders.

"Hold on," she told the boy. "Just a little farther."

She dragged him along the edge of the glacier. She dragged him over the wide swell of slippery boulders, his boots bumping along behind until, at last, she dragged him down the secret passageway hidden in the rocks.

And then - warmth!

A sultry, tropical heat that embraced them like a hug.

Sky stood blinking, letting her eyes adjust to the dim light of the cave. She was pleased to see that it was just as she remembered. The room was narrow and squat, barely higher than her head. The floor was flat except at its center where a shallow depression formed a pool. Filling the pool - bubbling up through a crack from the deep-down heart of the massif - there flowed a spring of clean, hot water.

Sky dragged the boy next to the pool. She twisted free from the backpack and placed it beneath his head for a pillow. The rocks were warm here, exuding a comforting heat.

"You should feel better soon," she told him.

The boy didn't respond, and Sky doubted if he would ever wake up at all.

Sky gazed at the boy's motionless shape before her, trying to think what else she could do to help. She crawled over and knelt at his feet, unlacing his boots and slipping them off one at a time with his wet socks. Sky lightly touched his toes. They were like ice. She did not know what she was doing, but she felt that it might help if she kneaded the boy's feet, coaxing some warmth down into his bones.

The boy lay unflinching through it all.

"Come on," said Sky, trying her best to sound cheerful. "Don't you want to wake up and say hello?"

But nothing.

Sky bit her lip, thinking, thinking, and then she nodded her head. She moved to his side. "Let's get you out of this sopping thing."

She leaned over him, fumbling with the zipper on his coat, pushing and pulling until it slipped sideways. "Ah," said Sky, nodding. "I get it."

She unzipped the front of the boy's coat, and then, like the petals of a flower, she parted the lapels.

"Oh!" she said, when she saw what lay underneath.

She sat back, her eyes wide.

"Oh," she said again.

The boy wore a sky-blue sweater. It seemed so odd to see that lovely shade of blue in the midst of such a gray stormy day. But more than that, woven into the wool over the boy's heart, there appeared a familiar design.

Sky reached out and ran her finger over the snowflake stitched with bumpy white thread. "It's you," she whispered, "It's just like you told me in the dream."

Her own heart filled up with joy.

"You're the snowflake like none of the others."

CHAPTER TWENTY-FOUR

LIFE, THOUGHT SKY, IS so very mysterious.

She was experiencing the profound suspicion that something, or someone - maybe the stars or moon - was working the pieces of a very big puzzle.

She was a piece.

This boy was a piece.

And the rocks and ibex and humans, and even each of the snowflakes, were all pieces, too.

And now, for some reason, within the midst of this tremendous storm, all of those pieces were quietly coming together to reveal life's magic in the most intriguing way imaginable.

"Wonderful," whispered Sky.

The boy continued sleeping beside the pool, and although he hadn't yet fully returned to life, Sky could feel in his hands that the warmth was slowly seeping back into his body.

"You're going to be fine," she assured him. "You just need a little rest."

She gazed into his passive face. A constellation of freckles sprinkled over the bridge of his nose and onto his cheeks. Sky liked looking at him. She was curious to know the color of his eyes. She wondered if he was dreaming. And if he was, Sky wondered if she played a part in that dream.

The storm continued to blow in the world beyond the cave. It dropped its improbable loads of summer snow over the massif, burying flowers and mountains alike. Sky imagined the statue of her mother, standing patiently on her mountain and covering with snow. Sky imagined her father.

The light grew dimmer in the room, until it became

completely dark with nightfall.

The hot spring bubbled in the darkness.

Water plinked musically from the walls.

Through it all, Sky could hear the voice of the glacier. It had been such a long time since she had any desire to sing along. She had felt so betrayed by the mountains and glaciers since they had taken Nan away from her. But tonight Sky sensed that life was not at all as she had come to believe. It was maybe not so lonely and tragic after all. It was quite possibly much more wonderful than anyone could possibly comprehend.

As she sat with the boy in the darkness, Sky began, very softly, to sing. She let that song rise from out of the deepest most mysterious regions of her soul. It felt so good as it moved up inside of her and filled the little chamber with its resonance.

Sky sang all through the night.

She sang until the blue-gray dawn returned to the cave, and she could see, again, the reassuring snowflake embroidered on the boy's sweater.

She sang as morning fully embraced the world.

And then the boy moaned. He rolled his head to the side.

Sky stopped singing and waited.

The boy licked his lips and grimaced. Slowly, blinking once - twice - he opened his eyes. He stared at the ceiling, focusing. Then he let his head fall gently so that he was peering directly into Sky's face. Sky couldn't help but smile. She had never known anyone with green eyes.

The boy knit his brow.

"Am I..." he managed.

But then he had to swallow at the dryness in his throat.

"Am I..." he said once more. "Am I dead?"

CHAPTER TWENTY-FIVE

SKY FELT SHE WOULD float away with happiness.

"No," she laughed. "You're not dead. You are alive."

"Oh," said the boy, and he touched the scrape on the side of his head, gingerly pressing it with his fingertip while sorting through the confusion of his sleepy thoughts. "Well," he said, "then I'm not really awake, am I?" He nodded slowly. "That's it. You're just a pretty dream."

Panic squashed Sky's joy.

"No!" she said. But as soon as the word left her lips, Sky realized it wasn't carrying the whole truth. "I mean, yes. I'm sort of a dream. Anyway, half of me is. But... Well..." She shrugged. "It's sort of hard to explain."

In fact, it was more than just *hard* to explain. It seemed downright impossible.

Sky realized she was talking to someone from an entirely different world. This creature hadn't been raised in the high mountains - that place where dreams come down from the sky. He was just a visitor here. And yes, they *were* speaking the same language, but he was speaking it from one side of the dream, while she seemed to be speaking it from quite the other. Sky had more in common with Tuff and Brownie, she sadly realized, than with this green-eyed boy from the lowlands.

"What's your name?" asked the boy.

"Sky," said Sky. "Blue Sky."

The boy grinned. "See what I mean? That's not a real name. Not for a person anyway. That's dream stuff."

Sky felt herself blushing.

The boy's grin faded. "Well," he said. "Even if you are a dream, it's not nice for me to make fun of your name. That's not what a noble explorer would do.

Especially since you saved my life. I'm sorry."

"It's okay," said Sky. "What's your name?"

"I'm Gaston."

"Gaston." Sky repeated the name and smiled. "That wouldn't be a very good name for an ibex."

"You know an ibex?"

"Of course. Lots of them." But she regretted it as soon as she said it.

The boy's grin returned. "See? People don't hobnob with ibex. You're definitely a dream."

"And you're a noble...explainer?"

The boy laughed, and then touched his head. "Oh," he moaned. "You're funny. No. I'm an explorer. At least I'm going to be. I'm just starting. Conquering The Steeple was supposed to be my first great adventure." He frowned. "But I guess that didn't work out so well."

"The Steeple?"

"The mountain where you saved me. Geez! You don't even know what it's called?"

Sky shook her head.

"It's never been climbed all the way to the top. The people in Étoile believe it can't be climbed at all. Some don't even think it *should* be climbed. But I would have made it," said the boy, "if it hadn't been for that darn storm. Then I'd be famous and rich, and I could buy a good sturdy sailboat and go exploring on the sea."

Étoile, sailboat, sea: Sky didn't really know what any of those things were. They sounded like words full of magic and mystery, wonderful otherworld words.

"It's good to be rich?" she asked. "And famous?"

"Heck, yeah!" said the boy. "Everybody wants to be rich. Then you can buy the stuff you want."

Sky nodded, pretending to understand. But honestly, what was *stuff* anyway? And why would everybody want it so badly?

"And so that's why you wanted to climb The Steeple? To get stuff?"

The boy raised himself onto his elbow. He tipped his head to the side and thoughtfully scratched the side of his nose. "Well, no. I guess not really. Not just for that, anyway."

He squinted at Sky, exploring her face and eyes, as if he were searching for something. Sky desperately wanted him to remember the shadowy dream where they had spoken. She wanted him to remember her. But her instincts told her it wasn't up to her to remind him. That's not how dreams are supposed to work.

"It's kind of hard to explain," he finally said.

"Sometimes when I think of climbing mountains, I get this funny feeling right here." He laid his hand on the snowflake over his heart. "It gets all warm inside of me, like I'm remembering something from when I was little, or... It might sound crazy, but it's like I'm remembering something from before I was even born. It makes me want to keep going up and up the mountain, no matter how hard it is. I don't care about anything else then, not stuff or sailboats or anything but climbing up and up."

The boy stared at Sky, recalling that wonderful warm feeling. Then he shook his head and grinned.

"Why am I telling you this anyway?" He lay back with his head on his backpack. "When I wake up it won't matter what we said. I'll probably just forget it all. That's usually what happens with wacky dreams."

Sky did not at all like being referred to as a "wacky dream."

"How come you're so sure I'm not real?" she asked.

"Because," laughed Gaston. "Real people don't belong in a place like this. And people sure don't make friends with ibex. Besides, look at you."

Sky looked at herself - at her arms and knees and body - but she didn't understand what he was saying.

The boy laughed again. "Nobody who's real can

survive in the mountains and snow like you do. You're like some picture in an old story book."

Sky struggled to understand. She shrugged. "What do you mean?"

"Heck," laughed Gaston. "You're naked as a jaybird."

CHAPTER TWENTY-SIX

NEVER - NOT ONCE IN her life - had Sky ever thought of herself as naked. She hadn't even known what it meant. But now, when Gaston told her that's just what she was, it was as if someone had turned over a rock under which that word - *naked* - and its meaning had been hidden all along.

"Goodness!" said Sky. She felt herself grow warm. She covered herself with her arms.

"I'm sorry," said Gaston. Blushing, he looked away. "I thought you knew."

Sky didn't know what to say.

An awkward moment passed while Gaston looked at the ceiling and Sky tried to decide what to do. She couldn't have felt more trapped had she been stuck half way up a snowy mountain.

Finally, while still looking away, Gaston raised up from his bed. "I know," he said, and opened the flap on his backpack. He reached in and brought out two bundles of cloth. "You can wear these."

Sky took the clothes. She ran her fingers over the bumpy fabric. Then she unrolled them, trying to understand how they worked.

Gaston glanced sidelong at her and the clothes. "They're climbing knickers," he explained. "Like mine. And my extra sweater. Go ahead and put them on."

Sky stood beside the bubbling pool, holding the green corduroy knickers upside down while studying how Gaston was wearing his. She struggled - first this way, then that. She got her toe stuck in a belt loop. Then she tried to stuff both her legs down one pant leg.

This, thought Sky, is the hardest thing I've ever done.

But after a little wrestling and readjusting, she managed to get the knickers on so they fit like Gaston's.

Gaston laughed quietly, trying not to watch. "Geez!" he whispered.

Once she finally mastered the knickers, Sky held up the black turtleneck sweater by the sleeves. She couldn't begin to imagine how to make this limp piece of cloth wrap her up in the same way that Gaston's sky-blue sweater was wrapping him.

"Here," said Gaston, and he slipped off his own sweater. "Like this." Slowly, so she could follow his directions, Gaston pulled the sweater back over his head. "Be careful not to get it backwards," he warned.

Sky did as he did. The sleeves were tricky - she got sort of twisted up - but she finally managed. Her head popped out of the correct hole; her arms were in the right sleeves - everything seemed to fit just right.

Gaston turned to face her. "Good job," he said. He helped her fold down the collar and pull out her long hair. "Perfect."

Sky rubbed her knuckles across her stomach, enjoying the wooly softness.

"You can keep them if you want," said Gaston. "As a present for saving my life."

Sky felt something wiggle inside her.

Stuff, she thought. I'm rich.

Sky smiled at the green-eyed boy who was smiling back at her. "Thank you," she said. "Thank you, Gaston."

"No problem." He knelt by his open pack. "I'm starving. Do you want something to eat?"

"Sure," said Sky, and sat down beside him.

Gaston pulled out two square tins and opened their lids. Sky was pleased to see they weren't filled with lichen or grass. He took a piece of something from one of the tins and put it between two pieces of something else from the other, then he handed it to Sky. He then proceeded to make the same snack for himself.

Sky didn't know how to approach the human food. She sniffed it.

"Geez!" said Gaston, shaking his head. "It's just bread and cheese."

"Oh," said Sky. "Sure."

"Like this." Gaston took a big bite out of his sandwich and chewed.

Sky did the same, and the instant the flavor hit her tongue, she trembled all over. It was so much better than ibex food! Somewhere hidden beneath that salty, grainy, exotic taste was the pungent faint flavor of milk. "Mmm!"

Sky said. She couldn't help herself. "Mmmmm!"

The two sat eating in the cozy cave while the storm continued blowing outside.

"It's neat here," said Gaston, surveying the room. "Is this your house?"

Not really knowing what a house was, Sky merely shrugged and continued to enjoy the sandwich.

Gaston dipped his fingers in the pool. "I could definitely live here."

"Really?"

"Sure. You got everything you need to stay warm. You can even take a bath. You just need a way to get food."

"You could stay here, if you want." That idea made Sky very happy.

Gaston examined the room, nodding. "Sure," he said. "I might do that sometime. Just live here and climb mountains. The perfect explorer's hideout. Maybe when I get back, I'll do that."

"When you get back?"

"From the sea."

Sky stared at him.

"Geez!" said Gaston. "Don't tell me you don't know what a sea is."

"Well," said Sky. "I've never seen one."

"Well, to be honest, neither have I. But I've seen pictures in a book." Gaston narrowed his gaze at Sky. "You do know what a book is, don't you?"

Sky blushed.

Gaston sat back on his heels. "Wow," he said. "Well. A sea is a big stretch of water. It's all salty and sometimes it has islands. Islands are pieces of land that rise up out of the water." The boy grabbed up a rock and placed it in the shallow part of the pool so that half of it was above the surface. "Like that," he said. "Only imagine the rock is as big as a mountain. And the water - the sea - is as big as..." He screwed up his face, trying to think. "Imagine it's as big as the sky.

Sky could almost see it in her mind. "Goodness," she whispered. The world suddenly seemed so huge - much bigger than the massif.

"I'm going to explore the sea," continued Gaston. "Maybe I'll get a job on a boat. I'll find old statues and sunk treasures, and I'll sell them for lots of money."

"And then you'll be rich?"

"Heck, yeah! I'll be the richest man in the whole world."

Sky didn't really know how many men, or boys, or

even how many people there were in the world. She figured there must be quite a few, at least more than there are ibex in the mountains. And so she felt quite privileged to be sitting with the one who was going to be the richest.

"I'll leave next spring, right after winter," said Gaston. "I'm making plans."

"Plans," repeated Sky, and she realized that *plans* were something she lacked.

Gaston stuffed the last bite of his sandwich into his mouth. He found his canteen and offered some water to Sky. Then, after taking a big gulp of water himself, he rummaged in the depths of his pack, pulling out a square of silver foil. "Ah," he said. "Dessert."

The boy peeled back the foil and exposed a dark brown square. Sky had no idea what it was. Gaston broke the square in half, presenting one of the halves to Sky. Then he put his own square in his mouth and sucked.

Sky looked at Gaston; she looked at the square in her palm. It had a little symbol of some kind of animal stamped into it - something most definitely from another world.

"That's just a cow," said Gaston.

Sky nodded. "Cow." She lifted the square to her

nose, sniffed its smoky sweetness, and then poked it into her mouth.

"Oh!"

Sky's eyes grew large with joy and wonder.

"What," she asked, "is it?"

Gaston smiled. "Geez!" he laughed. "That's crazy!" He grinned at Sky while shaking his head in disbelief. "Don't tell me you've never had chocolate."

CHAPTER TWENTY-SEVEN

THIS, DECIDED SKY, IS the most wonderful day of my whole life.

The chocolate turned to goo in her mouth, its sweetness melting through her entire body and causing her to shudder with pleasure.

Gaston watched, still grinning and shaking his head. "You're kind of weird," he said. "But I like you."

"I..." said Sky. (The chocolate momentarily glued her

tongue to the roof of her mouth.) "I think you're nice, too."

Thoughtfully, Gaston stood, stretched, and wandered around the little room, placing his hands on the warm granite walls. "Too bad this is just a dream," he said. "You're a really good climber. You and me could probably be pretty good friends."

"Why can't we be friends anyway?"

The boy shrugged. "Beats me. That's just not how it works."

"Why not?"

"Because then everything would get turned upside down. Imagine how mixed up the world would be if dreams came true and ibex sailed in boats on the sea." He laughed. "Everything has its place. And besides, dreams don't really exist anyway."

"That's not very fair," said Sky. "How come you get to exist, but not me?"

"Well..." Gaston gazed into the pool, tipping his head to the side. "Well, I just mean you don't really exist until someone believes in you. So, if you don't exist, it's kind of hard for you to be my friend."

"Well I believe in you," said Sky. "So why don't you believe in me?"

Gaston stared at Sky, his green eyes meeting her eyes of sky blue. "I don't know." He touched the bump on the side of his head. "I hit pretty hard when I fell. Maybe I'm just a little bit dizzy right now." He sat down with his back against the wall and closed his eyes. "Maybe I just need to rest."

Sky sighed. She had never had a more frustrating conversation, not even with her dream-talking mother. She tried to be patient. Gaston was, she had to remember, a guest and a stranger here. He could not be expected to understand the world of the high mountains. And he *had* almost died. It had to be kind of confusing for him, even if he was a noble explorer.

Sky ran her fingers over her knickers. She held out her arm and felt the soft wool on her sleeves. Yes. Maybe everything had its proper place in the world. Brownie would certainly look ridiculous if he wore a turtleneck sweater. But *she* didn't look ridiculous. Not at all. She just looked like a person. Perfectly natural. Maybe, thought Sky, I'm more like them than I ever imagined. Maybe they *are* my real herd.

That idea caused her to smile.

"What's funny?"

"Oh," said Sky. She hadn't realized Gaston was

watching her. Suddenly she wanted to learn everything she could about the world beyond the massif. "Tell me about what books are," she said. "And boats."

Maybe if she knew more about that odd world she could somehow become a part of it. Then surely Gaston could find it easier to believe in her.

"Please," she said. "Tell me what is Étoile."

Gaston laughed. "You're funny," he said. "But nice."

And so, as the storm continued to rage outside, Gaston told Sky what she wanted to know. Each question led to a hundred more. He told how villages were made of buildings - which is what people live in - and some villages were so big and made up of so many buildings they were called cities. He told her about the fish in the sea. He explained deserts that were made of nothing but sand and sky.

"Instead of ibex," he said, "deserts have camels."

"Camels." Sky repeated the exotic word under her breath. "Camels."

Then Gaston told her how he once had lived in an orphanage with some other boys who didn't have parents, but now he was an apprentice to a man who was a stone carver in Étoile.

"His name is Master Dujardin. He makes headstones and statues and the like. He's an alpinist, too. He's the one who taught me how to climb. He's very nice, but he knows I would rather be an explorer than a carver. I'm just saving my pay until I can leave for the sea."

Master Dujardin had given Gaston an attic room at the top of the building where he had his workshop, and it was there that the boy made his many plans.

It was difficult to imagine all that Gaston was describing for her. After all, Sky had no experience with anything beyond these mountains. But the boy was so enthusiastic, and so thorough with his explanations, that she was soon able to picture a sort of magical world in her mind.

It was all very beautiful and exotic, and certainly quite mysterious. But how, Sky could not help but wonder, was Gaston's world any less of a dream than hers?

CHAPTER TWENTY-EIGHT

SKY COULD HAVE LISTENED to Gaston forever. His voice was like a kind of boyish music, and so much cheerier than the drone of the glacier. But the stormy day passed all too quickly.

Gaston squinted across the room. "It's getting dark," he said. He turned and dug again in the depths of his pack.

Sky knelt beside him, eager to see his next people-world surprise.

The boy drew out a small canister that he twisted and pulled apart, doubling its length. He stood it on the floor. The bottom of the canister was silver metal, but the top half was transparent.

Sky bent and held her hand behind the curved glass, wiggling her fingers. Except for air and water and ice, she had never known there were other see-through substances in the world.

"Here we go," said Gaston.

Sky examined the tiny twig he held before her face. It had a bead of red at one end. Of course, Sky couldn't begin to guess what it was.

Gaston pressed the tip of the twig against the floor, and then, with a bit if drama, he scratched it sideways across the stone. With a spark and a little puff of smoke, the end of the twig bloomed with bright flame.

"Oh!" gasped Sky, and then she laughed because she just couldn't help herself.

Gaston grinned. He tipped the canister to the side and slid the burning match into a slot in the glass, touching it to a string. The string caught fire, and the boy withdrew the match and blew it out. He placed the glowing canister on a shelf on the wall. "There," he said.

The room filled with warm yellow light.

"Is it..." Sky knew she was going to sound silly, but she had to ask. "Is it a piece of a star?"

Gaston laughed and considered the light. "Sort of, I guess. It's called a candle lantern."

Sky leaned close to the lantern, watching the flame waver on its wick. "It's pretty," she said. "It looks like a flower."

Gaston nodded and yawned. "I always sleep with a candle burning." He glanced at Sky and hesitated. Then he spoke softly. "Well, I guess I can tell you that."

He lay back with his head on his pack. "I only remember one thing about my mom," he said. "I was pretty little when she died, so I only have one real good memory. She's putting me to bed," he said, "tucking the blanket up under my chin. And she's smiling. I can mostly just see her smile in the candlelight." He nodded. "She had a real nice smile." He looked at Sky, studying her face. "Like yours."

Sky felt herself blush.

"Do you ever talk to her in your dreams?" asked Sky.

Gaston yawned again and peered into the ceiling. "Beats me," he said. "I never really remember my dreams."

Sky felt a pang at those words. They caused an ache all around her heart.

Gaston turned onto his side. "But maybe it will be different with you," he said. "You seem sort of special. You seem like you might be someone I will know. Maybe you and me will sail the seven seas together, or cross a desert." The boy yawned one last time, and closed his shining green eyes. "Goodnight," he said. "Goodnight, Blue Sky. Thank you," he mumbled, "for saving my life."

"Goodnight, Gaston." Sky felt like she was saying goodbye.

She whispered his wonderful name once more. "Gaston."

But she knew he was already asleep.

CHAPTER TWENTY-NINE

IN THE MIDST OF that storm-ridden night, in the heart of those mighty mountains, snuggled deep in that cozy little room of stone, Sky watched over Gaston as he slept.

Candlelight flickered across the ceiling; it cast warm shadows along the walls.

The pool, like a watery lullaby, bubbled and splished and swirled.

Sky couldn't guess what was to come next. She suspected more surprises awaited. She hoped they would be pleasant surprises, full of Gaston's laughter and green eyes, but she feared they might be dreadful instead. Sky most definitely sensed dread lurking beyond the edge of her happiness.

The problem with stuff, Sky had already discovered, is that once you get it, you're in danger of losing it.

It was the same way with friendship.

"Maybe friends are just another kind of stuff," Sky told herself.

After all, Tuff and Brownie had gone away.

And Nan - she had just slipped away like a dream.

So right then Sky decided that maybe a girl was better off never tasting chocolate or friendship in the first place. Then you don't find yourself hungry for it when it's gone.

Sky sighed. "But it's too late for that," she whispered.

She recalled that first delicious bite of chocolate.

She could almost imagine Nan's soft fur against her cheek.

But most of all, she could still hear the echo of

Gaston's voice as he told her about the wonderful world waiting beyond the massif.

She wanted more of all these things.

Sky peered into the sleeping boy's freckled face. She knew the memory of his mother's smile was important to him. She had heard that in his voice. It was something he would always remember and be searching for. In fact, it was probably the very thing he had been speaking of when he told of that funny feeling he had in his heart when he climbed. It haunted his dreams. And it was what would someday inspire him to explore the blue sea. But the only real treasure he was seeking - the only one that truly mattered - was his mother's candlelit smile.

Surely it's the same for everyone, thought Sky. We are all looking for something we've lost - some friendship or dream - even if we don't clearly remember it when we're awake.

Sky thought of her father climbing The Steeple. What had driven him to try such a stunt? She thought of her mother watching him from across the canyon. Was her smile part of her father's dreams?

And then, in the next instant - quick as a flash of lightning - Sky thought of Old Stone.

It was as if she were suddenly hovering above him in

the darkness. In her mind's eye she could see the weary old animal huddled on a slope blowing over with snow.

"Oh," said Sky. She was ashamed she had let him slip from her thoughts for so long. She knew he was in a bad way, battered and abused by the storm.

"He needs me," whispered Sky.

But then she looked again at Gaston. She didn't really know if Gaston needed her, too. She hoped, selfishly, that he did, but she suspected otherwise. After all, he was safe now. He was out of danger.

Sky bit her lip, trying to decide what to do. She wanted to be here when the boy awoke. She had imagined her own smiling face to be the first thing he would see when he opened his eyes in the morning. Maybe then he would find it easier to believe in her. Perhaps just having him see her once more in the dawn would cause him to remember his dreams and somehow make her more real.

But the vision of Old Stone - his broken horn, his shivering body - wouldn't leave Sky alone.

The glacier's song rose above the music of the pool. It moaned a deep down moan that vibrated through the stones. Sky felt it pass through her own body. She felt it tremble through the mountains, announcing that one of their own was nearing the dangerous edge of a dream.

Sky bent over Gaston.

He laughed once from the depths of his own happy dream, and then muttered something Sky couldn't quite understand. She bent closer, turning her ear toward his lips, hoping to hear her own name.

But all she heard now was the candle in its lantern. It sputtered once, hissed, and in the next moment, it burned out, washing the room in darkness.

Sky laid her hand on Gaston's arm in that darkness, listening for a moment to his breath.

She turned away.

She had to go.

CHAPTER THIRTY

OLD STONE LAY IN the falling snow, his legs tucked beneath him, his head bowed, patient and still as his namesake.

Sky could just make out his silhouette in the darkness. She feared she was too late, that her weary old friend had already left this world behind. But then she saw him flick an ear. She moved closer, kneeling at his side.

Sensing her presence, the animal slowly turned his head. Even in the darkness, his golden eyes held dim flames of light.

"Ah," he said weakly. "You've come. Thank you."

Sky swallowed at the sudden dryness in her throat. "Of course," she said, trying her best to sound cheerful. "Surely you didn't think I was going to let you enjoy this lovely night by yourself."

The beast chuckled softly, and coughed.

Sky didn't know what to do next. Stone looked so small, more like a child ibex than a full-grown buck who had once been leader of the herd. At first Sky was taken aback. Then she began gently brushing the snow from his fur. She sat close to him, wrapping her arms around his neck and kissing him on the nose.

"Where did the summer go?" asked Stone. "This was such a pretty hillside when I first found it. So many flowers." He sighed. "Sometimes the mountains seem too harsh a world for such delicate things. Those tiny blossoms seem so out of place. But I've always appreciated the flowers and blue sky. What a dreadful place this would be without them."

"They'll be back," said Sky. "This storm can't last forever."

Stone nodded. "And what about you?" he asked. His voice had grown hoarse. "Will you be here, too?"

Sky was suddenly conscious of her sweater and knickers. They separated her from the animal world. She felt almost embarrassed to be seen in them, the same way she had been embarrassed to be seen naked by Gaston. But then she remembered Old Stone's kindness. Of everyone, he was the most understanding of her dilemmas.

"I don't know," she finally answered. "I'm still not really sure where I belong."

Old Stone was silent for a moment, the snowflakes ticking against his horns, then he said, "I feel sometimes that I have done you a disservice. I always felt you had a destiny with us, but I wonder if I should have delivered you to the valley that first night, to the people world, where the humans might have taken you in as one of their own." He paused. "I guess I just didn't know how to do that. At the time, that seemed as unlikely as depositing you on the moon."

Sky listened without speaking.

"Your father," continued Stone, "was the only human I ever felt I knew, and he was not like the others. He was as much an ibex as a man. So it seemed appropriate to raise you as an ibex, too."

Old Stone looked wearily at Sky. "But now you have grown," he said. "What I should have done, and what I did, are of little importance. You are becoming a young woman." He smiled in the darkness. "Now you will have to find your own way."

An immense heaviness settled over Sky as she realized the truth in Stone's words. She understood it was just part of growing up, and she knew she needed to be strong in ways she hadn't yet been. It scared her a little bit. It was like arriving at the hardest pitch on a climb. Sky saw there was nothing to do but be brave and face her challenge.

"I'll be fine," she said, although her voice quavered slightly when she said it.

"I am sure you will," said Old Stone. "You are an extraordinary girl. I am delighted that you came into my life when you did. As Nan often said, you were an unexpected gift from heaven."

The old animal let his eyes close. His head dropped and he seemed to fall asleep.

Sky held him close. There was so much more to say, and, at the same time, there was nothing left to say.

It was understood that Old Stone loved her very

much.

And Sky loved Old Stone.

The snowflakes continued to fall over the dark mountains.

The glacier moaned its otherworldly song.

Occasionally, Stone would mutter something in his delirium. But Sky knew it wasn't for her. She was not in his dreams now. He was dreaming the sunny, flower-laden dreams of his youth.

"I have grown old, mother," Stone said softly. "Even older than you." He tilted his horns to the side, and asked, "How can that be?"

And then, as if to answer the old animal's question, the clouds parted in the sky.

The storm, at once, ceased.

Like a wash of milk, the heavens filled with stars.

"Oh!" gasped Sky.

They were so beautiful!

Sky sat with her arms around Old Stone, peering upward.

Thank you, said the stars and mountains. It came to

Sky in the language of dreams, carried on a chorus of voices. *Thank you for being his friend.*

With her face still tipped to the stars, Sky nodded slowly, marveling at the immensity of it all.

Then she turned back to Old Stone.

She hadn't noticed that his head had settled to the ground, that his broken horn was buried in the snow.

She hadn't noticed that his breathing had stopped, and that, after such a long life, Old Stone had finally left the world of the high mountains very far behind him.

CHAPTER THIRTY-ONE

BY THE TIME SKY was back on her mother's summit, the sun was high and hot. The snow was melting fast. Water flowed in dark streaks down the granite face of The Steeple.

Far below, in the center of the boulder field, Sky spied the entrance to the hidden room. No steam was rising out of the rocks, but Gaston had marked the cave with three flat stones stacked one on top of the other.

Of course, he had gone.

He had awakened, forgotten his dreams, and continued on his way. That, at least, was what Sky assumed; it was what she most feared.

She could see the blue trail of his footprints in the snow. He had worked his way along the moraine, then dropped down into the distant green valley of Étoile.

Sad, happy, hopeful, uncertain: Sky suffered all of these emotions at once. They churned inside of her, creating a melancholy numbness all around her heart.

Sky knew Old Stone was in a better place. She would miss her old friend, but she was glad for him.

And she understood Gaston belonged in the lowlands.

But she still didn't know about herself.

A very large part of her wanted to follow the boy's trail down out of the massif and into his people-world life. What a wonderful dream that would be. But some nagging suspicion told Sky that it was not yet time.

"No," she whispered. "That wouldn't be right."

There was something else she had to do first, some task left incomplete, although she had no idea what it might be. Only the stars and mountains knew for sure, and they were secretive and unforthcoming.

She was pleased Gaston had marked the cave with a cairn. Surely that meant he intended to come back. But whether it would be soon, before winter, or many years from now, after he had explored the sea, Sky had no way of knowing.

Patience, said Sky's mother. *Patience like a stone is patient.*

But Sky didn't say anything.

She just squinted into the distance, straining to see Gaston's footprints as, one by one, they melted away beneath the summer sun.

PART FIVE

CHAPTER THIRTY-TWO

THE SUMMER SNOW LINGERED in the couloirs and on the shaded sides of the peaks. It dwindled, creeping in at the edges, but it never completely disappeared before the weather turned cold enough to preserve its patchy remnants.

The days grew shorter, the shadows longer.

Autumn arrived with a bite.

Sky watched the frosty boulder field in the dawn, her breath rising in little clouds before her blue eyes. She hadn't wandered far from her post since that morning Gaston had gone away. She would often stand for hours, motionless as a statue, watching in the direction of Étoile. Sky understood that it was an unlikely hope she held onto - it was getting too late in the season for humans to venture into the high mountains - but it was the only hope she had. And so, like a fallen climber, Sky clutched to her hope as if it were the fraying end of a rope.

Still, with each day, the boy's return seemed less likely.

Although she knew it was rather weak as far as plans go, her only plan so far was to have patience. (Gaston, the greatest planner she had ever met, would probably laugh if he knew.) But Sky herself had no real experience with planning. After all, she had been raised by ibex. They may be subject to a plan - one created by the mountains and stars - but ibex themselves do not make plans.

That, Sky decided, is the biggest difference between

animals and people.

People plan - to climb mountains and make statues and build houses, to sail the seas and find treasures - but ibex only react to the seasons. Sky desperately wanted to learn how to plan. If she could not, then how could she ever be fully human? And if she could not be human, surely she would never belong in the human world with Gaston.

So Sky resolved to teach herself how to plan, and then she decided that her first real plan was, indeed, to actually form a plan.

She let her shoulders slump, and sighed. "That," she mumbled, "is truly pathetic. You're going to have to do better."

She blew a plume of steam from her lips and let her gaze drift upward.

An eagle soared in the blue sky over The Steeple. It turned in broad circles, floating effortlessly on the invisible wind. Its shadow flashed over the sun-washed cliffs.

Sky had never trusted eagles. They always meant trouble. They plucked newborn ibex from their mothers; they flew just ahead of bad weather. And they always stirred in Sky the slightest feeling of dread. So when Sky saw that eagle, and when she felt that first dreadful tremor, it conjured all of her other dreads at once. It drew forth one dread in particular.

The human words of *purpose* and *destiny* were not in Sky's daily vocabulary, but she knew what they meant. She knew for sure how they felt. Since Stone had died, Sky felt very strongly that there was a reason she was here, some small but important part she was to play in the big plan, although she still didn't know what it might be.

Surely, thought Sky, that's why Stone brought me to the world of the ibex instead of the world of the humans.

As the eagle's silent shadow passed over her, Sky knew the time for her to discover that purpose had finally arrived.

She shivered, bracing herself.

In the next moment, coming up behind her, Sky heard the familiar sound of hooves clopping over stone. She turned to see a handsome pair of bucks bounding toward her up the slope. They were working hard, heads down, almost running, but when they spied the girl, they both stopped short.

Only a few yards separated the animals from Sky.

Unsure and wary, the beasts stood panting, foam at

the corners of their mouths.

One buck glanced at the other, nodded, and then stepped closer.

"Blue Sky?" he asked.

His voice was quite deep, but Sky heard something in it she knew. It called to mind games of tag, and echoes of laughter.

"Tuff?" she said. "Brownie?"

She was instantly self-conscious about her clothes, about appearing more human than ibex.

"You're so big!" she said. "And your horns are so long."

The three old friends stood staring at one another, none of them knowing what to do next.

"You're very..." Brownie stammered.

Tuff finished his brother's sentence for him. "Very pretty," he said.

Sky smiled. She stepped toward them. Then, in the same way she used to greet her playmates in the old days, she reached out and touched each of the young bucks on the nose. She was suddenly very happy, even with the dread still hanging in the air all around her.

"Why are you here?" She almost didn't dare ask. "Why have you come?"

Brownie peered sideways at his brother, then back to Sky. "We need you," he said. "Or rather..."

High above them, the eagle screamed in the sky.

Tuff drew a deep breath. "What he means," he said, "is that Tor needs you."

CHAPTER THIRTY-THREE

TOR!

The very name caused Sky to clench her teeth. The skin prickled on the back of her neck.

"How," she said softly, "could Tor possibly need me? I've not seen him since..." She paused, gathering her composure. "Since the day he sent us away."

Brownie shot a nervous glance at his brother.

Tuff nodded his horns. "We know how you must

feel," he said. "The ibex way is sometimes hard to understand. But in the end, it's all about what's best for the herd, Sky. Really it is."

This, thought Sky, surely can't be the reason Stone brought me to live with the ibex when I was a baby. Helping Tor *cannot* be my destiny. It cannot.

"Nan might still be alive," said Sky, "if Tor hadn't banished us. And Stone wouldn't have had to die alone if he could have been with the herd where he belonged." Sky glared at the pair of bucks and demanded, "How could that have been for the best?"

Tuff and Brownie waited before her, offering no answers, only hanging their heads.

"I'm beginning to think," continued Sky, "that the ibex way is just silly and cruel."

Tears pooled in her blue eyes.

The three stood for a time without speaking.

Finally, Tuff said, "Tor is our leader, Sky. He is the biggest and the strongest. For better or worse, he leads the herd. We need him."

And Sky knew, sadly, that what he said was true. There was no one to replace Tor. None of the other bucks were ready. Someday Tuff might be the one, but that time wasn't yet here. He was still too young. A herd with a weak leader was a weak herd, vulnerable, scattered, and lost in the wilderness.

"What about the way of the high mountains?" asked Sky. "I thought the ibex world and the human world were not supposed to touch and cross over." She stared at Brownie. "After all, I'm not really an ibex. You said so yourself."

Brownie cast down his eyes, but then he stepped forward. "No," he said shyly. "You are not an ibex. You're different. You're more like..." He stamped the stones beneath his hoof. He squinted into the empty air. "You're more like our princess."

Sky felt all twisted up inside when Brownie said that. She felt an avalanche of confusion spilling away inside of her. Placing her hand over her stomach, she stroked the reassuring softness of her wool sweater. Never had she felt so torn between worlds.

"What would Old Stone have done?" asked Tuff. "He was a great leader, even after Tor took his place. He always thought of the herd first."

That, too, was true, thought Sky. But then, Stone really *was* an ibex. And he had once been the actual leader of the herd. Sky recalled sitting with the old buck on his perch above the does and their young. She remembered the waterfall spraying over the rocks in a rainbow as the animals worked along, cropping the new grass.

Then, in the next instant, Gaston's voice came back to her - "People don't hobnob with ibex."

Sky turned and peered over the boulder field.

But where are you now, she wondered of the green-eyed boy?

Already, Gaston was beginning to seem like a dream himself. A wonderful dream, but still, in the end, nothing more than ether drifting away.

Sky sighed.

"What does Tor need," she asked, "that he can't take care of it himself?"

Tuff quickly explained the problem.

Sky listened, the glacier's low song drifting over the otherwise silent canyon. For some reason, she found herself thinking of Pebble. Sky remembered being small like that, when she was with Nan. She pictured herself playing in the flowers, before she had known her first winter.

"Where are you?" she whispered to Gaston. "Why don't you come back?"

She waited.

But the glacier's motherly song was the only sound.

"Can I ask you something?" said Sky to Tuff and his brother.

"Yes," answered Tuff. "What is it?"

Sky pulled back her hair and deftly wove it into a long, tight braid. Then she stood with her arms at her sides. "Do you believe in me?" she asked. "I mean, do you believe I really exist?"

Sky didn't dare turn to see how the bucks had reacted to her question, but she felt them staring at her back, trying to understand what she meant.

At last, Brownie spoke. "Heck," he said. "You're our best friend. How could we not believe in you?"

Sky closed her eyes, letting those wonderful words echo around in her mixed-up mind. Well, she thought, at least I exist for someone.

She opened her eyes and searched once more beyond the glacier and the boulder field, beyond the world of the high mountains to the distant valley. Nothing but rocks and ice and patches of crunchy snow lay between her and Étoile. Except for his tiny cairn, there was no sign that Gaston had ever been here at all. There was no reason to believe.

Letting her gaze drift over the canyon, Sky scanned

the base of The Steeple. She held up her hand, shading her eyes from the glare of the autumn sunlight.

"Okay," she said. "I have a plan. But I need your help." She nodded once, with conviction. "And I will need a strong red rope."

CHAPTER THIRTY-FOUR

THE CRAGS.

Sky had never laid eyes on these pinnacles of stone. Not once had she dared venture into this forbidden region of the massif. This was a realm - according to the ibex way - inhabited only by bucks. It was no place for does and their little ones, and certainly no place for a young girl who had been banished from the herd. Of all the far-flung corners of the world, this was the one where

Sky felt most confidently that she did not belong.

However, Tuff and Brownie now led her boldly into the very heart of that closed and secret world.

Sky followed her friends across the grassy hammocks between escarpments. She hopped the little streams burbling in the sunlight. This was an enchanted place, unlike anywhere else she had been, and still, Sky sensed a heaviness weighing in the misty air.

The trio climbed to some terraces above a slope of rocks. Sky carried the red rope in loops over her shoulder. She scrambled up a short stone wall, until, at last, the other bucks came into view. They all stood peering down the shaded side of the mountain.

Sky stopped short. Such a tangible gloom was cast over the creatures that it caused her to pause. The animals looked her direction, and Sky could see in the way they held themselves - in the slump of their shoulders, and the droop of their horns - that they were feeling lost. They appeared more like a gathering of little ones than a herd of mighty bucks.

Brownie turned to Sky. "Come on," he said. He was panting hard. "Over here."

The desperation in his voice was unsettling. Sky could hear his fear.

Sky braced herself, and then strode bravely into the center of the milling bucks. No one spoke, they only lifted their horns in solemn greeting. Sky met each animal's gaze, trying her best to feel courageous.

"This way," said Tuff.

Sky stepped to his side and then leaned out so she could see down the cliff.

A stretch of smooth, cold stone dropped straight away from the ridge to a narrow ledge strewn with rubble. Heart-shaped hoof prints scarred a few patches of snow. Hunched on that ledge, heaving with exhaustion, his muscles strained to failure, stood the once mighty Tor.

The beast was still for a moment, but then, sensing Sky's presence, he slowly, painfully, lifted his head and stared directly into her face. His swollen tongue jutted from between his lips.

A tremor passed through Sky when her gaze met Tor's. There was no mistake - it was a feeling of intense hatred. She hated Tor. She hated him for all he had denied her, for not accepting her when she was young, and for sending her away from her friends. But most of all, she hated him for the pain he had caused Nan and Stone. Sky steadied herself, reeling with hatred.

Tor gazed up from below. His expression was blank and beaten.

Sky glowered down at him, hatred coursing through her like nausea.

A mass of cold air hung thick as fog between the girl and the buck.

But then, quite unexpectedly, Sky felt something odd coming to bloom inside of her. Her hatred was being pushed away by something at once more gentle, and more powerful. It was an emotion she had never experienced before. It felt both alien yet friendly at the same time, as though it had been there all along, but had merely been hidden beneath deep snow. Now, peering down at the pathetic figure of Tor, Sky felt something akin to compassion. But more than that, she felt in herself a loss and a panic, as if she, too, were part of the herd now made vulnerable by Tor's impending doom.

Old Stone had once told Sky that her father seemed more like an ibex than a man, and now, in an instant, Sky understood that something of her father's connection to the mountains was rising to the surface of her own being. She was a girl, yes, and she was partly dream, but also, in a very big way, Sky understood - she was an ibex.

She caught her breath.

The revelation was almost too much for her to comprehend, too heavy for her to bear.

The herd's problems, she thought, are my problems as well. We're all part of the same dream.

And when the herd's leader was in trouble, when the herd's strength was threatened, Sky could not help but feel some of that same trouble in her very own soul.

The girl peered down at Tor. She trembled. She sensed Nan and Stone and her own mother and father and all the stars in the blue sky watching down on her. She felt, mysteriously, as if she were looking with them into a very important part of herself. She could certainly choose not to help.

She could just as easily turn and walk away.

"But no," she whispered. "Tor must be saved."

CHAPTER THIRTY-FIVE

SKY LIFTED GASTON'S ROPE from her shoulder and tied it to the end of a large block of granite above the cliff. She gave her knot a good tug, testing its strength. Then, with the line hanging in loose coils from her hand, she stepped back to the cliff's edge and tossed it out into space. One by one the red loops unraveled in the sunshine, the rope dropping straight down the shady side of the mountain. Sky peered down the cliff.

"Good," she whispered. The rope reached the ledge with a few feet to spare.

She turned to Tuff and Brownie. "Wait close," she said.

The bucks stood side by side.

Sky grabbed hold of the rope and, stepping backward off the ridge, she began descending hand over hand into the abyss.

The air was cold with glacier breath, the stone quite vertical and polished. Sky was surprised to find no cracks or holds of any kind. No matter how skilled a climber might be, without the aid of a rope, this cliff was unclimbable.

How peculiar, thought Sky, that a mountain-savvy creature like Tor should find himself trapped in such an inescapable spot.

Down she went, lowering herself slowly, carefully, until she was able to plant both her feet firmly in a crust of snow on the ledge. Still clutching the rope, she bowed her head, drew a deep breath, and, with all her nerve, turned to face Tor.

The big animal waited before her, his shins scraped and bloody, his golden eyes somewhat dry and listless.

Sky felt one small stirring of hatred, but then it

quickly passed.

"Hello, Tor," she said.

Tor only stared at her.

Sky gazed up the glass-smooth wall. It was such a long way to the top. A fall like that would have killed anyone else. Tor's strength had saved him. But now what? Below the ledge the cliff continued uninterrupted for another thousand feet.

"You've gotten yourself into quite a fix," said Sky. She examined the buck with her eyes. "Did you break any bones?"

He did not respond.

"How did you get here?"

At that, Tor laughed, and looked out over the canyon. He swallowed. "A flower," he said. His voice was rough as sand.

Sky didn't understand. "A flower?"

"A yellow one," continued Tor. "It was growing on the ridge, just over the edge. It's too late in the year for flowers. It seemed like a little treasure just for me. I thought I could easily reach it. I thought I would just have a little snack." He laughed dryly and turned back to Sky. "But," he said, "I slipped."

Sky nodded. She didn't know what to say.

The young girl and the battered animal stood facing one another without speaking.

A chill breeze blew over the shadowy cliff.

At last, Tor said, "When I was little, I had a sister. She was my twin. Her name was Fenn."

Sky found herself taken off guard by his words. It was all but impossible to imagine Tor as little. And she had sure never imagined him capable of telling anyone something so personal.

Tor stared into the rubble and snow before him, smiling slightly, as if he were seeing his sister once again.

"She was such a tiny thing," he said, "and so sweet. We played together." Tor rocked his great rack of horns, remembering that long ago time.

"But one day," he continued, "while we were napping in the grass, a shadow passed over us. I looked up, but the sun was in my eyes. I could not see anything except a dark shape in the blue sky. There was a rush of wind. And then nothing." Tor waited. He seemed to be reliving the experience. "I thought Fenn was still right beside me. 'Did you see that?' I asked her. But she didn't answer." Tor slowly shook his head. "The eagle had carried her away."

Sky held the red rope, waiting for Tor to continue.

He raised his head.

"I've tried to push that terrible day from my memory," said Tor. "But one does not forget such things. Whether you want it to or not, it comes back to you in your sleep." He looked directly into Sky's face. "I guess that is why I have always hated dreams."

Sky shivered. She felt Tor's hatred of dreams piercing to the very core of who she was.

"That memory has made me the buck I am today," said Tor. "It guided me to see the high mountains in a very distinct way." Again he peered wearily out at the canyon, and at the rugged mountains and glaciers surrounding the crags. "This is a hard world we live in," he continued. "There's no room for weakness here. Old Stone was right - you see things differently when your strength is gone. You see things a bit more clearly. Still, it does not change how things are."

Tor fell silent. He let his eyes close.

Sky placed her hand on the cold face of the cliff, considering what Tor had said.

Another breeze blew in over the canyon, and Sky knew from experience that it meant the arrival of yet another storm. What's more, she knew that Tor felt it, too. She sighed. There could be no mistake - winter was already coming fast.

"We need to get you off of here, Tor. Before the snow starts."

"No," answered Tor, and opened his eyes. "I'll stay here. It's the way of the high mountains," he said. "This is my end."

Sky gave the rope a little tug, following it with her eyes up the wall. "Well," she said, "that would certainly make it easier for me." She lowered her gaze to Tor. "But," she said firmly, "I'm afraid that's not going to do."

The big buck looked at her indifferently. He seemed unimpressed by her determination.

Sky let go of the rope and stepped toward him. She tried her best to look strong. "Not all dreams are dreadful," she said. "You've been foolish to think so. You've cut yourself off from some very wonderful things by believing that way. Besides," she said, "some dreams are here for a very good reason."

Tor appeared unmoved.

"There's something much bigger than you and your little problem, Tor. There's a big wonderful dream full of mystery and magic. You are part of that dream. So am I. And we both have a job to do." She stepped still closer. "The herd needs you."

Tor snorted. "It makes no difference."

"It does."

Tor shook his head.

"You know they'll struggle without you. A herd's leader is its heart."

"They will manage."

"They will perish."

Tor answered with silence.

"You owe it to them, Tor," said Sky. "It's your duty. You have no choice."

Tor looked away from her.

Shadows were now passing swiftly over the canyon floor, sweeping over the glacier and boulder fields. The blue sky was filling with clouds.

"Old Stone wouldn't have acted this way," said Sky. "He always thought of the herd first."

Tor kept silent.

Sky bit her lip and clenched her fists. She was becoming angry and impatient with this unmovable, arrogant, ignorant beast. But she knew she had to be careful. Too much was at stake.

"What about Pebble?" said Sky. "Isn't she like Fenn?"

Tor tensed.

And Sky saw that her words had touched him.

"What will happen to her this winter?" said Sky. "You could save her. Are you really going to let her suffer?"

Tor appeared to be at a loss. His dry eyes began, just slightly, to tear. That gave Sky courage. She took another step toward him.

"It will be fine, Tor," she said softly. "You know in your heart that this is how it must be. You just have to be strong in ways you have never been before." Sky leaned forward and, gently, laid her hand against the animal's neck.

The massive buck stood still. Sky felt him relax under her touch. She spread her fingers in his thick fur.

"Tor," said Sky. "It is time for you to accept your part in the dream."

CHAPTER THIRTY-SIX

PRESERVING TOR'S DIGNITY WAS going to be the most difficult part of his rescue. But Sky thought that a small blow to his pride might do him some good.

"Nothing wrong with a little lesson in humility," she whispered to herself. (It was just one tiny gesture of revenge for all the trouble he had caused her.)

Still, it was hard to see Tor in the same way she had before hearing his story of Fenn. So much had been explained about how he had always acted as leader of the ibex. And Sky found she could no longer muster a single ounce of the hatred she had once so intensely felt for the beast. That hatred had blown away with the wind. Sky was pleased at how much more free and light she felt without it weighing her down.

She gathered the extra rope and skillfully fashioned a double sling under Tor's chest and belly. The buck held still while she worked. He didn't speak.

Sky checked her knots and then stood before him. "Okay," she said. "I'll go up now."

Tor was rigid and panting in short breaths.

Oh, Sky realized, he's scared.

After all, it was not every day that an ibex is lifted out of trouble by a young girl. This was most definitely a case of the human world and the ibex world coming together, something Tor had disapproved of all his life. He had to feel at least a bit uncertain about this people-way of doing things.

"It will be fine, Tor." Sky smiled. "You don't have to do anything but hold still."

Tor bobbed his head ever so slightly.

Sky tipped back and peered up the wall. The clouds were growing thicker, blocking out the sun. The red rope stood out vividly against the gray granite. Sky took hold of the rope and climbed the cliff.

Tuff and Brownie were waiting on the ridge.

The other bucks held back a ways, curious and concerned, but cautious. They were too wild to ever feel comfortable around a human, especially one wearing knickers and a wool sweater.

After untying the rope from the anchor, Sky made two loops in the end of the line. "Come here," she said to Tuff and Brownie.

The brothers went to Sky, but when she held up a loop toward Brownie, he shied away.

"Come on," she said. "This will be fun. You get to show me how strong you are."

Reluctantly, Brownie bent forward so Sky could get a loop over his horns and neck. She pulled the rope down so that it was against his upper chest. Then she did the same with Tuff. The two bucks waited side by side with their rumps toward the cliff.

Sky stepped back to the edge and looked down. She gave the rope a little tug, and then laid it over the smoothest and roundest part of the stone rim.

Tor gazed up from below.

Sky held out a hand and waved.

The great beast lifted his horns once, signaling that he was ready.

"Okay," said Sky. "Steady. Start pulling."

As Tuff and Brownie leaned into the load, the slack rope between them and Tor stretched tight. The loops dug into the fur on their chests. At first they made no progress at all. Tor was just too big to budge.

"Pull harder," called Sky.

The young bucks dropped their heads, flexed their muscles, and dug more deeply into the rough footing on the ridge. They strained. They heaved. And as they placed one deliberate step in front of the next, Tor began, very slowly, to rise from the ledge.

"Good!" said Sky. "Just keep going."

Sky knelt on her hands and knees and watched over the edge as Tor was hoisted up the cliff.

"Keep pulling!" she called over her shoulder. "Go!"

Tuff and Brownie crept forward, winching Tor to safety.

Up he came. One inch - two - up and up.

Sky sat back on her heels, quite pleased. Her plan was working. Now, she thought, it's just a matter of minutes. She was already looking forward to the time after Tor's rescue, to when she would no longer feel that nagging need to accomplish her destiny.

Tor held himself perfectly still, just as Sky had instructed him to do.

She smiled to herself confidently as she followed Tor's steady progress.

But then, as if a shadow had passed over her, Sky felt herself go cold.

While peering down the precipice, it suddenly occurred to her that Tor was many times bigger than Gaston, that he weighed more than four or five boys lumped together, and that the red rope was too thin, too light, and not at all designed for the load it was being asked to haul.

Sky gulped.

Brownie and Tuff pulled and scratched for a footing, sparks jumping from their hooves over the stones.

Tor dangled like a sack of large boulders at the end of a thread.

"Oh!" said Sky.

The taut rope slid over the stone.

If it should break, thought Sky, Tor is lost for good.

And no sooner had she allowed that fatal thought to enter her mind than Sky spied a weaker length of rope passing over the stone lip. Its weave began instantly to fray; the rope began to jerk and pop as, one by one, each strand ripped apart.

There is a hanging moment right before a disaster when everything seems to pause. The earth stops spinning on its axis; the wind ceases to blow; the glacier stops its song. It's the thinnest fraction of time, almost immeasurable, when all the world becomes perfectly poised for catastrophe. Sky felt herself hovering in that slim and terrible sliver of time. She felt herself teetering on the brink of horror.

Sky stared wide-eyed at the unraveling rope.

And then, quick as a single heartbeat - ka-thump - the moment passed.

The rope snapped.

"No!"

She lunged forward and grabbed the severed ends of the rope, clamping them tightly in each of her fists.

Tor dropped a ways down the cliff.

Tuff and Brownie lurched.

And the sudden force of it all yanked Sky's arms wide apart.

It would have torn a normal girl in two; it would have ripped her arms from their sockets.

But although Blue Sky was normal in many ways, she had other traits as well. In that exact instant, calling on the deepest part of herself, Sky forgot anything else she might have been and became wholly a dream. Only in dreams could anyone perform such a feat as she did then.

Strung between the two lengths of rope, with Tor swinging in the air on one end, and Tuff and Brownie working shoulder to shoulder on the other, Sky allowed her body to act as the missing portion of rope.

"Go!" she called to her friends. "Pull!"

Tuff and his brother strained forward with the last of their strength.

Stretched in the middle, Sky shuffled sideways, the taut rope gripped securely in each of her hands.

Tor's horns finally appeared over the edge of the cliff. He stalled for a moment at the rim. But then, with one final grunt of effort, Tuff and Brownie heaved in unison, and the big animal's entire body flopped onto the ridge.

CHAPTER THIRTY-SEVEN

SKY COLLAPSED.

She fell in a pile on the rocks.

Everything went black, as if she were tumbling through a starless night sky. Everything became silent.

Slowly, painfully, the dream part of herself twisted and flipped and began to rejoin with the part of her that was flesh and blood. A roar sounded in her head.

"Ooooh!" she moaned.

Brownie's face came into focus before her. His voice seemed to be drifting from far away. "Sky?" he said. "Are you okay?"

"I…" Sky swallowed, "I think so." She wasn't entirely sure. She felt like she had just taken a ride in an avalanche. She felt as if her arms were on backward and her head was screwed on upside down. "I'll be fine," she muttered. "Just give me a minute."

Her face was resting on the stones. She could feel the grit beneath her cheek, but she couldn't seem to lift her head.

Every bone in her body seemed to be mending, and every stretched out muscle eased back into place.

"Oooh," she groaned again.

How could anything hurt so much?

She opened her hands, stretching her fingers out wide.

She shut her eyes tight, trying to squeeze out the hurt.

Sky would have lain like that for a while longer, just letting the pain subside, had it not been for the tremor she felt beneath her. Slow and deliberate, heavily thudding, the ominous tread of hooves came near, and then stopped.

Sky opened her eyes once more and then lifted herself onto an elbow, blinking upward.

The sky was close and gray and spitting snowflakes.

The wind was whipping over the ridge.

And towering above her, his arching horns seeming to snag in the clouds, was Tor.

The great buck no longer appeared pathetic and beaten as when he was trapped on the ledge. Now he was twice as big as ever. He looked broad as a mountain. He stared down at where Sky, quite small and girlish, lay trembling in a heap of twisted limbs and tangled hair.

Go ahead, thought Sky. Smash me flat.

She was in no position to do anything to stop him, but it did seem terribly unfair.

I know you hate me, she thought. So now is your chance to finish me off.

Tor stood without speaking. He loomed above her in the blustery air.

Sky waited for the end. She was sure it was close, although she had no idea how a part-dream girl could die. It sounded like a horribly messy and painful business.

Then Tor dropped his head down close to her, and Sky saw her own reflection bulging in his golden eyes.

"Take hold of my horn," said Tor. He dipped his head her way. "I will lift you up."

"Oh," said Sky. She struggled to her knees and wrapped her fingers around the broad shaft of one horn.

Tor raised his head, gently lifting Sky to her feet.

She held on for a second, until her dizziness had passed, and then she let go of Tor's horn and stepped away from him. "Thank you," she said. Self-consciously, she brushed the dust from her knickers.

The other bucks had all gathered in close. They stood in a half-circle around Sky and Tor. Tuff and Brownie, with the red loops still hanging from their necks, waited a few steps away.

Tor lifted his face to the wind, squinting into the snowflakes. He appeared to be thinking.

Sky stood swaying before him, the last of her pain melting away.

"I do not believe," said Tor, "that humans belong in the high mountains." He seemed to be speaking to the sky. "I do not believe that our worlds should touch and cross over." He nodded thoughtfully. "And I have never liked dreams."

Sky waited for him to finish. It felt as though he were passing judgment on her.

The big buck turned to her. "But..." He gazed at Sky for a moment, considering her, and choosing his words carefully. "But," he said again, "maybe I've been wrong." He then spoke softly so that only Sky could hear. "Maybe the world is more mysterious than I thought."

Sky smiled.

Tor bowed his head toward the girl, and then joined the other bucks.

Tuff and Brownie came over to Sky. They were grinning.

"You did it!" said Tuff.

"I knew you could," said Brownie. "I absolutely knew you could."

Sky lifted the rope from each of their necks and they vigorously shook their heads, glad to be free.

"You boys are strong," said Sky. "You're definitely mighty bucks."

The three friends laughed together on the windy ridge. Sky had never felt so light and happy.

"Blue Sky!" called Tor.

Sky and Tuff and Brownie all turned to the leader of

the ibex.

"Winter is coming," he said. "It is time for the bucks to go with the does and their young." Tor looked directly at Sky. "You are welcome to join us if you like."

Sky smiled, and raised her hand to Tor.

Then the huge buck turned and, followed by the others, began working his way down the ridge to start the long march back to the tarn.

"Will you come with us?" asked Brownie.

Sky laid her hand on his neck and stroked his fur. She shook her head. "Not now," she said.

She turned and squinted into the stormy distance. She could not see The Steeple through the rolling clouds and snowflakes, but she knew right where it was. She could see it in her mind. She thought of Gaston's cairn.

She thought of his green eyes.

"Maybe I'll come later," Sky said to her friends. She kissed them each on the nose. "But right now I have something I need to do."

CHAPTER THIRTY-EIGHT

THE STORM HAD BEEN blowing for some hours by the time Sky returned to the boulder field. The day was ending. Gaston's cairn was already buried under snow.

Sky dropped to her knees and scooped with her fingers to exhume the squat little tower of rocks. She admired it in the waning light. She imagined Gaston building it, balancing one stone - just so - on top of another. But in no time the snow began covering the primitive sculpture again.

With a sigh, Sky turned to the entrance of the cave. She gazed at the crooked opening in the rocks.

Gaston had been here while she was off rescuing Tor. Sky knew it was true. She recognized the lingering people-world scents of his damp sweater and of skin washed clean with soap. She even believed she could hear, if only faintly, the echo of his voice calling her name.

"Oh, sure," said Sky. "I step out for one single day and *that's* when you decide to pay me a visit."

She squinted up into the veil of falling snow. "By now," she said, "I suppose you are already back in Étoile." She held out her hand. "The snowflake like none of the others."

The cold snow piled on top of her head.

She did not know what to do.

It took all of her effort not to cry.

Sky stood and descended into the room.

"Well," she said. "If I can't be where you are, at least I can be where you were."

It seemed a pitiful consolation.

The cave was nearly dark. Sky had to let her eyes adjust to the dimness. Then the room began to reveal its details. First she saw the walls and low ceiling. Then she saw the warm pool glimmering in the center of the floor, and the place next to it where Gaston had lain while recovering. At last she saw the narrow shelf where the boy had once placed his lantern.

That's when Sky felt her heart jump up to her throat.

She leaned forward, trying to see.

The shelf was still there, yes, of course it would be. And the lantern, of course, was gone. But...

Her eyes widened.

She almost did not dare move. She did not want to ruin the wonderful trick she felt her mind was playing on her. But then she stepped - floated really - across the narrow room.

She stood before the shelf, drying her palms on her knickers.

Drawing a deep breath, she reached out and, carefully, laid a single finger on the large silver square she found glowing bright as a star in the near-darkness. Her finger glided over the slick foil wrapper. She knew just what it was. She lifted it to her nose and sniffed.

"Mm!" she said. "Chocolate!"

A tremor of joy passed all the way down to her toes.

Then she turned her attention to the other item on the shelf, an object far more intriguing and weird. She laid her palm on the cool cloth cover. Then, recalling how Gaston had once described it to her, Sky opened the pages and let them flip beneath her thumb.

They made a pleasant rustling sound in the hollow chamber of the cave.

Although it was nearly dark, Sky could just make out the shadowy shapes flitting before her as, one by one, the pages spilled their marvelous images into her hungry imagination.

The book fell open to one page in particular, and Sky found herself smiling when she realized what she was seeing.

"Oh!" she said. "Camels!"

PART SIX

CHAPTER THIRTY-NINE

CAMELS AND DESERTS AND cities and seas with islands and fishes and boats.

Page after page.

The book proved to be a veritable treasury of dreams.

During those first stormy days of winter, nestled down in her cozy refuge, Sky had never felt so rich. She perused the colorful pictures while nibbling slivers of chocolate. She enjoyed the wooly warm luxury of her sweater. And, just as Gaston had once suggested, she began thinking of the stone room as her very own house.

(She tidied it up a bit, sweeping out the gravel and moving two large rocks so they were arranged like chairs next to the pool.)

Still, it was not so much her actual possessions that made Sky feel wealthy; it was that Gaston himself had given them to her. After all, he had returned to the cave to bring her the book and the chocolate bar. Didn't that mean he believed in her?

Isn't that, she asked herself, proof enough that I'm real?

"Yes," she answered herself hopefully. "Surely it is."

She nodded her head for emphasis, as if to scare away her doubts and make her realness just a tad more real.

There was no question that her own existence was the best gift of all, but now that Sky had it for certain, she wasn't quite sure what to do with it.

She turned to the book, scanning its pages for answers.

On one page she found the picture of an enormous

church, complete with gargoyles and stone angels. Sky laid her finger on the paper and traced the shapes. What weird, wonderful things!

On yet another page was a field of cows. They all wore bells around their necks. They had large brown eyes. Sky smiled. Those sway-bellied creatures appeared far too fat to ever climb mountains.

Although Sky had always thought of the world as a puzzle, she was now beginning to see that puzzle as much more vast than she had ever guessed. Each mountain was a piece of that puzzle, to be sure. Each dune and its individual grains of sand, each winter storm with each of its snowflakes, each bird and flower, and even each boy and girl were all parts of the whole. Not to mention the ibex and their cumbersome cousins the camels and cows. That and so much more. But what made the puzzle so incomprehensible was that each of its pieces was a puzzle unto itself. It seemed every little thing was a dream suspended like a cloud within the biggest dream puzzle of all.

"It never ends," whispered Sky. She had turned to a picture of a woman walking with a little boy beside a river. The woman balanced a large clay jar on top of her head. "It's like the stars."

For some reason, that realization made Sky feel both very happy and very sad at the same time. It caused her to feel alone while also feeling that she could never truly be alone. "It's the song of the glacier." Sky said it aloud to the room. "It's Gaston's candle." She wasn't entirely sure what she meant by that. The glacier's song had always been full of that same happy-sad feeling.

Sky put the book away and knelt beside the pool. She dipped her fingers into the warm water, swirling them slowly in the bubbles while softly humming.

"I wish you were here," she said, speaking to Gaston. "I would like to talk to you about this."

But the green-eyed boy had been drifting farther away from her. Sky never felt herself moving in his dreams anymore. It was as if in meeting her dreamer, and becoming more real, she had, in part, ceased to be a dream.

Sky stood and walked to the entrance of the cave. Of course it was snowing. It hadn't stopped for days. She held out her hand so that the snowflakes landed on her open palm. As they lighted on her warm skin, they turned to tiny beads of water.

She closed her hand into a fist and pulled it back into the room.

She closed her eyes and imagined herself walking through a summer field of cows, touching each one on the nose and saying hello.

"That's what I want to do," she whispered.

And just maybe Gaston could be there, too.

But the distance between her and that dream seemed very far right now - as far as the chasm between being awake and being asleep.

CHAPTER FORTY

AND THEN ONE DAY she ran out of chocolate.

Sky suffered a shiver of panic when she realized.

It wasn't that she was so desperate for sweets. She had lived her whole life without chocolate until meeting Gaston, and had survived just fine. But it was more what that empty wrapper seemed to mean - it felt like she was moving in the direction *away* from Gaston and his world.

Sky folded the foil in half and placed it inside the book next to a picture of the sea. Then she glanced across the room.

A beam of yellow light leaked into the cave at the entrance, indicating that the massif was enjoying a sunny break between storms. The ibex, on their south-facing mountainside, would be stretching their legs and soaking up the warmth. Sable, Pebble, and Brownie and Tuff. A deep longing seized Sky when she thought of her friends. It would certainly be nice to have some company.

"No," she said. "That's not where I'm supposed to be."

She felt another destiny lay in store for her, although she suspected only the stars knew what that secret plan might be.

While absentmindedly weaving her hair into a braid, Sky wandered across the room and stepped through the doorway into the sunshine.

"Oh!" gasped Sky.

She was met with such a dazzling scene. After so many dismal days underground, the sunshine filled her up with unexpected relief. Like a sun-hungry flower, she lifted her face to the light and smiled.

She scrambled up onto a snow-covered boulder and,

shading her eyes with a hand, squinted down the glacier to where it disappeared toward Étoile. She sighed, thinking again of Gaston. Then she turned and looked up at the mountains looming in all their grandeur against the blue sky.

The Steeple.

And directly across from it - her mother's lovely peak.

It had been a long time since Sky had paid her mother a visit. And climbing sounded so enjoyable on such a perfect winter day. So she set off.

Only it was so much harder than Sky remembered. Her mother's mountain - a fairly easy peak to climb - seemed so much trickier today. She nearly slipped twice. Her fingers ached. And she found herself unable to perform even the easiest moves. She simply didn't have the strength.

What's happening to me? she asked herself.

It was late in the afternoon by the time Sky finally gained the summit. She rested bent over with her hands on her knees, sucking big gulps of air.

When at last she caught her breath, Sky stood and turned toward her mother, trying to smile as if nothing were wrong. "Hello," she said.

The woman didn't respond. She stood in her statuesque pose in the snow, a mound of white fluff resting on top of her head.

Sky stepped closer, peering into her mother's impassive face. She brushed the snow from her head and shoulders. Then Sky took hold of the woman's hands.

How cold they were!

Sky fought her rising panic.

"It's me," she said. She found it difficult to speak the language of dreams. The words seemed to come out sideways and jumbled. But then Sky sensed, very slightly, the tiniest bit of warmth in the woman's fingers. That gave her reassurance. Sky leaned closer. "Are you there?"

I am always here, answered the woman. *But where are you?*

Sky was taken aback. She wasn't sure how to answer. And her mother's voice was so soft and garbled, barely audible, as if it were coming from over a great distance.

"I'm here," shouted Sky. "With you!"

No, said the woman. *You are not. I hear it in your voice. You have begun a journey. You are already on your way.*

Sky laughed nervously. "That's silly."

No, said the woman. *You are where your heart is, and that place is not here.*

Sky felt the truth in what her mother said. A tightness gripped her throat. "Oh," she whispered. "I'm sorry."

The woman laughed softly. *It's fine,* she said. *It is as it should be.*

The sun was already low over the horizon, turning the mountains and the statue golden with alpenglow. The brief winter day was ending.

Night was speeding forward.

Overcome, Sky began to cry.

She sobbed for a time while holding the stone woman's hands.

The sun slipped away.

Finally, the woman said, *In some measure, we all begin as a dream. But not everyone is meant to stay that way.*

Sky struggled to understand her mother's words. They sounded farther and farther away.

Something inside of you is waking, said the woman. *Now you must decide...*

Her voice trailed off, as if becoming part of the breeze.

"Decide what?" asked Sky.

The woman stood motionless before her. If she was speaking, Sky was unable to hear.

"I must decide what?"

Do you belong in the dream...

Sky leaned closer, turning her ear toward the woman's mouth.

...or do you belong on the other side?

Sky shook her head. "I don't know," she said. "Tell me."

The woman was silent as stone.

"Mother!"

But it was no use. Sky knew she was now farther than the stars.

CHAPTER FORTY-ONE

AN ENORMOUS BONE-WHITE moon rose into the night. All but the brightest stars were washed away by its brilliance. The mountains, so solemn and still, leaned shoulder to shoulder in the moonlight. They cast long shadows over the canyon.

Sky sat hunched on the mountaintop, the night air crackling with frost all around her. She held herself wrapped in her arms, but she couldn't keep from shivering. It was annoyingly distracting. She was, after all, trying to form a plan.

To help her concentrate, she focused her gaze on the far away lights of Étoile. They were like the tiniest stars in the farthest galaxy.

"Or at least they may as well be," she muttered.

Such a treacherous expanse lay between here and there.

But somewhere down there, by the light of one of those tiny stars, Gaston was going about his evening. Maybe he was having supper with Master Dujardin. Or maybe he was poring over a map, or reading a book about sailing. Sky nodded. She tried to guess which star was his, but decided she could not. Winking through one eye, she held up her hand, aligning it so the distant village appeared to be resting on the tip of her finger. How fragile it seemed, like a cluster of snowflakes in danger of melting away.

Old Stone had once warned her that the people-world might not be habitable for ibex. He warned it might be guarded by dangerous beasts. He said the air was too thick to breathe. So was that why dreams seemed always to dwell in the highest mountains, close to the sky?

But it's getting harder to breathe here, too, thought Sky. She recalled her winded climb earlier in the day. And until tonight, she had never had problems staying warm. No. There could be no doubt - she was undergoing a change.

"So what am I turning into?" she asked the moon.

But the moon drifted in the heavens without comment.

Sky was overcome with a fit of trembling. Her whole body felt as if it were being shaken by invisible hands. When it subsided she stood stiffly, stomping her feet and slapping her arms in a futile effort to keep warm.

After a moment, Old Stone's voice came back to her from long ago. "You may have to fend for yourself someday," he said. "You'll have to find your own way."

Sky hadn't fully understood what he meant back then, but now the old buck's words struck her with a truthful force. She listened harder, trying to hear more, hoping to remember something else that might be of help.

But there was only silence.

Her mother was silent; the moon and stars were mute; even the glacier stopped singing its song for her tonight.

"Oh," whispered Sky. "I see."

She suspected she wasn't truly alone. Surely she was not. But never in her life had Sky felt so much as if she were. Never, she realized, had she been quite so afraid.

"Well," she said bravely, "it doesn't matter, does it?"

No one answered.

Sky stood on the mountain in the night. She sensed that she lacked something important - some vital tool, or quality - something, at least, that she needed very badly in order to do the crazy thing she now felt herself about to do. But she was getting too cold to think clearly. Time was running out. That essential something eluded her.

"Oh, well," she told herself. "Maybe it will come to me."

Of course, she had her doubts, but she couldn't really wait any longer. She peered into the sky and, speaking to all the invisible friends she hoped were listening, she said, "Wish me luck."

Then she set off for Étoile.

CHAPTER FORTY-TWO

THE SNOW WAS DEEP and soft.

As Sky trudged beside the glacier, she began for the first time to grasp the wisdom of the ibex approach to winter - if you weren't going to migrate to the valleys below the storms, then surely the next best thing was to climb up to the wind-scoured peaks. But this whole region in between was ridiculous. So much snow! Sinking up to her waist, Sky felt as if she were wading through an endless sea of snowflakes.

She struggled along, the moon hovering over her shoulder like a watchful eye.

At least I'm going downhill, she told herself. (She was doing her best to stay positive.)

It was such hard work that she had to stop several times to catch her breath. But each time she did, the ice immediately began to creep into her bones until she was forced to keep moving.

Finally, she lost enough elevation for the snow to become less deep, only up to her knees, and Sky was able to travel more quickly. Leaving the glacier and mountains behind, she broke over a crest and dropped into a forest of pines. They cast tangled shadows over the ground.

Sky had never seen trees up close before. She placed her palm on their rough bark. She touched their needles, bending to smell the sweet pitchy fragrance.

The silent shadow of an owl glided past.

A band of deer bounced away through the trees.

Already, this world was so exciting and new. Sky could have spent all night just wandering through the forest.

"But no," she assured herself. "There will be plenty

of time for that later."

She blew her warm breath into her hands and gazed down the slope through the dappled moonlight.

A dog barked in the distance.

A shiver ran up her spine; she knew she was getting close.

She emerged from the trees onto a narrow road. It was nearly free of snow, with only a few patches of packed ice on the corners where the low winter sun couldn't melt it during the day. Stepping cautiously into the middle of the road, she peered first to where it bent out of sight behind a short hill, and then in the other direction, toward the sound of moving water.

Sky nodded resolutely. "This way." And she walked fast, even though she was scared.

The road soon crossed a stone bridge that spanned a raging river churning with ice and foam. The waves splashed silver beneath the moon. Once over the bridge, Sky came to the first house.

Squat and humble, it sat nestled back in a stand of trees. It was clad in whitewashed plaster with a split-shingle roof covered by a cap of snow. A lazy sigh of smoke breathed from the chimney. The little house had only two windows, both dark, spaced like eyes on either side of the front door, giving it the appearance of a blank face. Sky was curious, but she snuck by. Surely the house was too small to be a stone carver's shop. And it wasn't tall enough to have an attic.

Soon she came to another house - and another - and then another, all side by side in a row down the road. There were no trees now. They had all been cut down. And the houses were more grand, some with two or three stories, and many windows. Since it was the middle of the night, and their occupants were sleeping, the houses stood silent in the moonlight. Sky pictured the sleepers in their beds - men and women and children snuggled beneath heavy quilts. That certainly sounded more pleasant than traipsing about in the cold.

Compared to her own home in the boulder field, these houses were extremely fine. Sky felt somewhat embarrassed when she realized. She had been so proud before. But her house was really just a hole in the rocks, more like a peculiar burrow, she realized, than what anyone would call a house.

As she moved closer to the heart of Étoile, Sky began

to sense she wasn't alone. She stopped, cocking her head to the side. She looked up. A whole host of dreams was floating in the air above the smoky streets. Sky couldn't see them, or even hear them, but she felt them there drifting over the rooftops. They passed like ghosts, hurrying down from the mountains to join their dreamers.

How much am I like one of you? Sky wondered. And even more tonight, how much am I not?

Sky knew she was still stuck somewhere in between, neither here nor there. But she wasn't yet sure if she was becoming more like a sleeper about to wake, or more like a dream about to vanish into oblivion with the dawn.

She shook her head. She didn't have time to stop and think about that right now. She was on a quest. Such thoughts would only undermine her courage and determination. And she felt nothing would change anyway until she found what she was after. So she kept going.

More buildings followed. More and more, and bigger and bigger. Streets and alleys began branching off from the main road, dividing the rows of buildings like narrow, twisting canyons. A few streets had tall poles with dim bulbs glowing on top. They cast pools of cold electric light over the sidewalks.

Some of these buildings, Sky began to realize, were not houses at all, but different kinds of shops.

One had tall windows behind which headless mannequins posed in long coats.

Another shop sold flowers. Sky pressed her nose to the glass, looking into the dark interior lined with vases and bouquets. It seemed so odd to see flowers blooming in winter, as if the little room was holding summer captive.

In yet another shop, Sky saw rows and rows of colorful skis leaning against a wall. The opposite wall was dedicated to climbing gear: ropes, clips, boots, and ice axes.

Then Sky was drawn to the most inviting shop of all. It gave off a heavenly aroma. Floury loaves and cakes were displayed in its front window. A bakery. Gaston had told her about those. Sky felt a sharp pang in her stomach when she imagined the taste of warm bread. She licked her lips.

But as wonderful as these shops were, as full of promise and mystery, they were not what she was looking for. She stepped back into the empty street, gazing in all directions.

"Where are you?" she whispered. "Where can you be?"

And then, as if in answer to her question, from the deep shadows of a dark alley, a dog growled.

Sky froze.

The invisible creature grumbled a threat in a language Sky didn't know. There was a sound of heavy breathing. More growling. And then the dog barked.

Sky did not wait to see what the dog had in mind. She bolted in the opposite direction. She didn't know where she was fleeing to, only that she wanted to get away fast.

She rounded a corner, glancing over her shoulder. She suddenly felt so out of place, so not of this world. She ran blindly down the streets, like a scared wild animal. Panic gripped her as one street appeared exactly the same as the last. It seemed she was running in circles, lost in a maze.

Finally, out of breath, she forced herself to stop.

Sky bent over, panting. Her whole body trembled and heaved. "Oh," she said. She struggled to regain her sense of direction, and her daring.

Étoile was just too overwhelming. There were too many corners and bends leading to nowhere. This whole adventure seemed suddenly hopeless. As with climbing a mountain, Sky had reached the hardest pitch and continued forward. But here it made no difference; she was just too unskilled to proceed with any hope of reaching her goal. She would have felt more at home had she found herself trapped halfway up The Steeple in the midst of a violent storm.

But then, very soft, and from far away, Sky heard her mother's voice. She held herself still. Sky didn't know if she was actually hearing those words - if her mother was truly speaking to her in this very moment - or if she was merely remembering those words now when she needed them most. But it made no difference. All that mattered was that Sky let those soothing sounds come into her and take hold with their meaning.

Listen, said her mother.

And Sky listened, tipping her ear to the sky.

Listen with that part of yourself that knows how to hear.

Sky stood, pulling back her hair and squaring her shoulders. She tried to remember how to do as her mother had once taught her. First, she closed her eyes.

At once, a calm settled over her. She listened more closely. Soon, reassuringly, she heard the rising, gentle thump of her heart.

The moon whispered into her ear.

She heard the song of the glacier.

The far away mountains whispered her name.

At last, through it all, Sky heard another heart beating in time with her own.

She drew a deep breath, and turned.

The first thing Sky saw when she opened her eyes was a statue of a beautiful angel. Her moonlit wings were open and raised, her face made sad with shadows. The angel stood before a building with unmarked headstones leaning against the wall in the snow.

Then Sky noticed an even more intriguing sight. It felt as if she were peering into one of her own forgotten dreams, or perhaps the very dream from which she had been born. Over the front door of the shop hung a relief. It was carved of the same white stone, and it glowed softly in the moonlight.

"Oh!" gasped Sky. The sculpted figures were so oddly familiar.

First, shaggy and ragged, there was an old ibex standing on a ledge.

And then, perched on top of his head, her tiny hand grasping the base of his broken horn - a naked little girl.

The girl smiled down at Sky

Sky felt herself swoon.

She held her hands to her sides to steady herself.

Then, as she gathered her wits and balance, Sky lifted her eyes higher, up and up the building. All the windows were frosty and dark. All but one.

Way up there, at the very top, a little peaked dormer had been built on the side of the roof. The window on the dormer was aglow with a wavering yellow light. It seemed almost to breathe and laugh.

Sky felt herself grow suddenly nervous, and suddenly happy.

All of her fears began flying away.

"Ah!" she whispered. "A candle!"

CHAPTER FORTY-THREE

THE FRONT DOOR OF Master Dujardin's shop was tall and wide. Sky pushed on it, but it didn't budge. She grabbed hold of the handle, giving it a tug - nothing happened. So she stepped back into the street.

Trembling, she held herself tight, gazing up at the candlelit window.

The little girl sitting on top of the ibex smiled down at her.

The angel stood nearby.

"I don't suppose you could just fly me up there?" asked Sky.

But if the angel answered, Sky was unable to hear.

Sky nodded, and blew a frosty cloud from her shivering lips. She studied the situation, searching for a reasonable route to the window. The building, one of the tallest in Étoile, was six stories high and covered from top to bottom in smooth plaster. Although the windows each had a narrow ledge, they were spaced too far apart to offer any holds that Sky could reach. Then she spied the waterspout. It was fastened to the corner of the building and ran all the way from the ground to the gutter at the edge of the roof.

Sky squinted at the spout. "Maybe."

She recalled her earlier climb up her mother's mountain. The very thought of it caused her to sway with fatigue. She sighed. She knew she wasn't the climber she used to be; she was changing. But, she asked herself, what else can I do?

Sky peered up to where the moon was slipping out of sight behind the rooftop. At the moment, that roof and the moon seemed to be about the same long distance from the earth.

"Oh, well," she whispered, and walked to the corner of the building.

She swung her arms, loosening her shoulders. She rolled her head from side to side and rubbed her palms together. Then, taking a deep breath, she wrapped both of her hands around the metal pipe.

"Goodness!"

It was like taking hold of an icicle.

Sky knew she had to hurry. Her fingers were sure to grow numb and loose their grip. She lifted a foot and placed it flat against the wall. Then, leaning back, she flexed her whole body, raising her other foot to the wall on the opposite side of the pipe. The metal creaked under the strain, but straddling the waterspout in this way, Sky began her strenuous climb to the roof.

She immediately settled into a shuffling rhythm. One hand slid a ways up the pipe - then the opposite foot - then the other hand - on and on. Her back and arms pulsed with pain, but Sky ignored it. The ground slowly receded below her.

Don't look down, she told herself.

All of her thoughts were on going up, up.

Just as her strength was flagging, and just as her fingers were stretched to their limit, she came to a heavy iron bracket attaching the pipe to the wall. Twisting into position, she stood on the bracket and rested. She wrapped her arms around the pipe and cupped her frozen hands over her mouth, filling them with warm breath. The feeling came back into her fingers with the sensation of pins and needles.

Sky leaned out, assessing her progress. She was about half way. She couldn't see the window on the roof. She couldn't see the moon. But moonlight shined in the streets and on the other buildings, so she trusted it was still there.

The cold pipe continued straight up the wall to where it bent at an angle beneath the eave and connected to the gutter. Wiggling her fingers, Sky took hold of the pipe again, and climbed.

Up she crept.

Slowly.

Carefully.

The sidewalk below was now far and hard. She didn't dare slip. At this height, such a mistake would be the end of her.

"Camels," she grunted. "And sailboats."

With each step up the wall, she added another image from her book.

"Cows."

It helped her to concentrate.

"Islands...

"A lady with a jar on her head...

"A little boy...

"A river..."

Until, at last, she reached the gutter.

Again, Sky was able to rest on an iron bracket. But this time the eave was too low for her to stand, so she cowered in the angle between the pipe and the roof. Squatting on her heels, she assumed the hunkering pose of a gargoyle.

Her roost was cramped and cold and her muscles immediately began stiffening with the night air. She shivered violently, not sure if it was a chill, or a sudden upwelling of fear. She peered down the dark wall to the sidewalk - such a long way!

Sky slowly shook her head. "At least I know I won't be going back that way," she whispered. She couldn't imagine finding strength enough to shimmy back down that pipe.

Then she craned her neck and tried to see up over the gutter. But she couldn't. What lay beyond was a hopeful mystery. She was at the irreversible crux of the climb. There was no way down, and only one dubious way to the top.

"Well, Blue Sky," she muttered. "You've done it this time."

She would have liked to have taken a longer rest, but it wasn't a very restful place to be. Besides, good or bad, she was eager to see how this night might end.

Uncurling her body from its perch, she held onto the pipe with one hand, while reaching out with her other. She stood half bent over and, while still facing the building, leaned away from the wall. Her hand grasped at the empty air behind her head, clutching at nothing - nothing - until at last her fingers found the edge of the gutter. She grasped the frigid metal flange. Then, for a long moment, she waited, her feet pressing into the plaster wall, her arms stretched wide between the pipe and the edge of the roof.

Sky understood she couldn't stay in this strenuous position for long. She was too tired, and growing more so by the second. But she was struggling with her courage. There had been a time when she would have easily, and without any doubts, jumped into the athletic move she was poised to perform just now. But that time seemed like it had occurred in a long forgotten dream. Could any part of her being even remember how to do such a thing? Could any part of her ibex upbringing, her father's alpine legacy, and her mother's dreamy ways come together and help her now when she needed them most?

There's only way to find out, she finally concluded.

So she let go of the pipe and shot her hand out to take hold of the gutter.

One foot came away from the wall.

And then the other.

Sky swung back and forth, back and forth, like a rag blowing in a soft breeze.

Her arms stretched painfully above her head.

Briefly, she considered her choices. But she quickly realized she had only one option left.

"Oh, wonderful," she huffed. Then she began to swing her body from side to side, each swing growing slightly higher than the last.

"One...

"Two...

"Three...

"Go!" she cried.

Her leg swung in a high arc out to the side; her foot floated, for an instant, above the roof; and then her heel came down lightly and hooked on the lip of the gutter.

She hung like that only for an instant, gathering herself for the next move. Then, with a heave, a grimace, and a desperate twist, Sky squirmed her body over the gutter and onto the edge of the roof.

CHAPTER FORTY-FOUR

FROM SOMEWHERE ACROSS THE village, a dog barked.

Another dog, his voice ringing with an unmistakable tone of menace, answered from the other direction.

Sky listened, lying on her back, watching her glittering breath dissolve into the air above her face. She held her body rigid against the gutter.

"Ooooh!" she moaned.

Gently, bracing both of her feet against the metal trough, she sat up. All the rooftops of Étoile were now spread out before her, washed in pale blue moonlight. Sky leaned out and peered over the edge. The stone angel was far below, her eagle-like wings still raised as if poised to take flight, but now the angel was immersed in the shadows cast by Master Dujardin's building. From this angle, the relief sculpture of the little girl and the ibex was no longer visible.

Sky turned and looked up the roof. She was glad to see the moon again. It seemed to warm her with its light. But still more than that, she was pleased to finally be so close to the dormer.

"Just a ways more," she told herself, and she could hardly believe it was true.

Sky punched her fist into the crusty snow, testing its strength. The pitch was steep, but the snow was hard enough for her to kick good solid steps, and Sky moved easily up the slope until, at last, she found herself kneeling before the window.

Sky held her hand over her beating heart. This window, she realized, is the star like none of the others. How many times had she seen it from the high mountains without recognizing it? The thought made her smile as she anxiously leaned toward the glass and peeked in.

The room was small, its ceiling sloped and low. A map of blue oceans covered the opposite wall. Beneath the map was a shelf loaded with books. A pair of mountain boots rested beside the shelf, and beside them - a backpack.

"Ah!" said Sky. She had seen that pack before.

Her eyes were then drawn to the candle. Having burned all night, it was no more than a stub sinking into a saucer of its own melting wax. But the flame - quivering like a yellow flower - was still bright enough to light the room.

Placing her fingertips against the frosty glass, Sky let her gaze drift at last to the boy-shaped lump buried in blankets on the cot. His back was turned to her, but of course she knew just who it was. She felt the word forming on her lips - "Gaston."

Then she said it again - "Gaston."

It was right then, in the very instant of whispering his name, that Sky sensed herself teetering on the utmost edge of a dream. She was very nearly to the end of her journey, on the verge of leaving one world behind for another. Only a single move separated her from the other side. It should have been an easy enough move to make. After all, it was no more than a matter of rapping her knuckles against the glass, waking her dreamer, and having him open the window to let her in.

But Sky faltered.

She felt that something more than a pane of thin glass was blocking her way, although she couldn't say just what it was.

She bit her lip, feeling all of her courage drain out of her at once, and all of her self-confidence.

And as any climber knows - just as her own father had learned on the day he fell from The Steeple - hesitation in the midst of a crux move can be fatal.

Long and low, a blood-chilling howl rose to Sky from the street.

It was instantly joined by another, then another, and another.

Then, all the dogs of the village - Étoile's self-appointed guardians - began frantically barking at the rooftop.

Startled, Sky turned to the sudden racket in the

street. When she realized the disturbance was directed at her, she gasped.

"Hush!" she hissed. "Quiet!"

But that only excited the dogs more. They snapped their teeth and jumped into the air, as if hoping to reach her and tear her from the roof.

"Please be quiet!"

But the dogs were a determined bunch, eager to wake the village and alert it of this odd, nocturnal intruder.

Sky leaned toward the window, her palms against the glass. She considered breaking it, but wasn't sure how to do it. Inside, she saw that Gaston was still sound asleep. The clamor outside hadn't yet penetrated his dreams. Then she heard a gruff voice from below.

"Who's there?"

A man was standing in the street in his pajamas.

In the same instant that Sky saw him, the man's eyes met hers. They glistened in the moonlight.

For a long moment, the man seemed to be gathering his thoughts, trying to comprehend just what it was he was seeing - a girl on a high roof? It was too improbable. It was too absurd. Then Sky saw his posture change as his mind seemed to leap to the only sensible conclusion he could find.

"Stop!" he called. Then louder, with the dogs gnashing and barking all around him - "Thief!"

Terrified, Sky whirled from the window. She jumped up and ran at an angle across the roof, gaining speed. She didn't know where she was going. She had no plan for what to do when she ran out of roof. She only knew that she needed to get away.

The dogs barked in the street.

The man shouted.

And Sky, having reached the end of her run, did the only thing that she could do - like a young and brave-hearted ibex, she leaped into space.

CHAPTER FORTY-FIVE

IT WAS THE STARS who came to her rescue.

Or some magic in the moonlight.

Sky suspected it was so, even as she sailed through the air.

How else could she ever have crossed such a distance? She didn't have the strength to do it herself; she was no longer dream enough for that. Surely some invisible hand had caught her mid-leap and was carrying her from one high rooftop to the next.

The whole world held its breath.

The cold air turned warm as a hug.

The wide alley passed dreamily beneath her feet.

And then, just as she neared the end of her leap, everything came rushing back to speed.

"Oomph!"

Sky crashed into the snow and rolled down the roof. One somersault led to another, her limbs flying in all directions, her body tumbling wildly out of control. Had she not lunged for the chimney as she passed, desperately clutching for a handhold of brick, she would have continued over the eave and into the street full of dogs.

Her arm jerked straight as she slid to the end of her reach. Her sinews stretched like rubber bands, her finger joints popping.

"Ahh!" she winced. But Sky held on.

The dogs went mad with excitement. Another person had joined the pajama man in the street - and then another - and together the three shadowy figures were all waving their fists and shouting over the noise of the dogs.

"Come down here, you!" they cried. "Thief! Police!"

Sky scrambled behind the chimney, crouching out of sight. First she glanced one direction - the way she had just come - toward Gaston's window. As much as she wished to be back there now, and as much as she already regretted leaving him behind, she didn't dare try that leap again. So she turned the other way.

The buildings were closer together on this side of the alley. Thank goodness the gaps between appeared more manageable. Quickly picking a route, Sky darted from her hiding place and fled over the rooftops.

The dogs chased after her.

Sky ran and ran, her feet pounding through the crusted snow, jumping and hopping along the ridges and smoldering chimneys.

The dogs, although moving fast, were now at a disadvantage. Whereas Sky could turn any direction she needed, the dogs had to navigate the winding streets, finding their way around buildings and walls. The pack soon began to unravel, a few animals running one way, a few more circling around from another side. All of Étoile seemed to be filling with the raucous yapping of dogs.

Sky followed the route of least resistance. When an alley appeared too wide to jump, she automatically turned in another direction. Sometimes she was able to climb a short wall to a higher roof, but more often she found herself only going ways that led downward, leaping from higher roofs to those that were slightly lower. She soon found herself losing height until she was no more than two stories above the street.

And then she reached the end of the village.

Sky stood panting and looking down. A river flowed along this edge of Étoile. She could hear the water moving more swiftly downstream, but directly below her the river had slowed to form a wide pool. Ice crept in from the edges, but at the pool's center was a space of water that was still as a glass window. In the center of that calmness floated the tranquil reflection of the moon.

Sky briefly considered her choices. She looked over her shoulder, toward the center of Étoile, but she knew that people were gathering there. Their shouts carried in the night.

She leaned out and peered down the smooth plaster wall, searching for handholds - but there were none that she could manage.

The dogs were getting closer, following her scent through the winding streets.

Sky gazed up at the moon. It was exactly the same bone color as the stone statue of her mother. That gave

Sky a bit of hope. That made her feel not quite so alone. "Well," she whispered to anyone who might be listening. "Here we go again."

Sky nodded and took three long backward steps on the roof ridge. She stopped, stooped a bit at the waist, and clenched her fists.

The dogs howled in the streets.

And then Sky sprinted to the edge of the roof, leaping once again into the magical moonlight.

CHAPTER FORTY-SIX

SPLOONSH!

Sky splashed down in the center of the moon, shattering it into a million pieces. And then she was surrounded by a burbling darkness. Her head filled with a hollow silence, her hair floated in a fan around her face, and for a second Sky found herself quite confused.

Have I landed in the river? she asked herself. Or did I truly leap as high as the stars?

She felt for sure she was drifting in outer space.

She soon realized she was mistaken. It wasn't the stars she sensed watching her from all sides, but the silvery eyes of trout. They blinked out from the shadows under the ice. It was a surprisingly peaceful place to be. So quiet. No one was chasing her down here. And after working so hard against the forces of gravity, it felt so relaxing to be weightless.

But then Sky felt the current that ran in the depths of the pool. It grabbed at her ankles, trying to drag her down. Her lungs began to burn. She sighed underwater, a few bubbles of spent breath escaping through her nose.

You can't rest just yet, she told herself.

And so, leaving that peacefulness behind, she kicked hard to the surface.

"Ahh!" she gasped, her head emerging from a ring of ripples.

At once, the baying of the dogs resumed. They were closing the distance. A wall of moonlit buildings brooded over the river's shore, and the more persistent of the dogs were just on the other side, searching frantically for a passage to the water's edge.

Sky knew the chase wasn't over yet.

There was too much ice along the far bank to make an escape that way, so she rolled onto her stomach and began stroking downstream. The pool gathered and swirled and emptied into a narrower channel where the water began to move more swiftly. The roar of the rapids below soon grew louder than the din of the dogs upstream.

The waves grew taller and more violent as the stream dropped away on its course. After taking a slap of water in the face, Sky learned to time her breaths with the up and down bucking of the waves. But the rapids tossed so wildly, it proved difficult to do, and in no time she found herself gulping for air.

Like a scrap of driftwood, Sky felt herself at the mercy of the river.

The current gained more speed.

She bounced off of rocks, scraping her knees and elbows.

She dropped over falls into churning whirlpools that wouldn't spit her out until thoroughly tumbling her in a bath of icy foam.

On and on it went.

Vaguely, Sky began to feel that she might be drowning. She needed more oxygen than she was getting. She was taking such a beating, and her mind had grown fuzzy and numb. Exhausted as she was, she almost let herself go to it - almost gave herself up to that watery death - when she found herself lifted high on a surging wave. For a hanging instant - just before the wave collapsed beneath her - something caught her eye. It glowed unusually bright in the moonlight. She recognized it at once - the bridge!

It was the very bridge she had crossed when she had so hopefully entered Étoile earlier in the night. From somewhere in her waterlogged brain, Sky was able to piece together all that that bridge might mean for her now.

If I can get there, she told herself, then I can get to the road. If I can get to the road...then the forest...then the mountains...then...

She had no time to formulate any thoughts beyond that. The bridge was coming up fast. She knew she had to act.

Sucking down one last gulp of air, Sky began beating her arms and legs in the roiling water. All of her efforts were on getting to the bank beneath the bridge. She slammed sideways into a rock, taking a blow to the ribs, but she kept stroking across the rapids. She went under once more, the current clutching at her clothes, but that only made her all the more determined. (After all, Gaston had given her that sweater.)

You can do this, Sky! She silently shouted encouragement to herself. Believe you can do this!

And all at once, she did believe.

Something broke free inside of her and she believed in herself in a way she never had before.

An unreasonable strength surged through her every cell, a lingering dream strength that seemed to wake and take her over.

Sky gritted her teeth, and then, with one last mighty kick, she heaved her battered body onto the narrow shelf of ice at the river's bank. It crumbled along the fringe, but the ice proved thick enough to hold her weight.

Sky wiggled out of the river into the shadow of the bridge.

CHAPTER FORTY-SEVEN

NOW SHE WAS ON her hands and knees, belching up river water, and quivering with exhaustion. At once her hair froze in a tangled mass of clinking tendrils. Her sopping knickers grew stiff in the bitter air. But worst of all, Sky felt the water turning to a glaze of ice over her skin. It seemed that Death itself was taking hold of her, encasing her.

"No," she muttered.

Although it came to her as no more than the thinnest shadow of a thought, Sky understood that she *must* keep moving.

Struggling to her feet, she dragged her body over the snow-covered rocks and up the bank. When she finally reached the road, she collapsed again, gasping for breath.

Sky lay with her eyes closed until, through the fog of her confusion, the piercing howls came to her over the noise of the river.

The dogs had reached the pool.

Dimly, she imagined the frenzied animals milling at the river's edge, trying to sniff out which direction their quarry had fled. As much as she wanted to rest a while longer - as much as she would have enjoyed taking a little nap right there on the bridge - Sky did not at all like the next image that came to her - the one in which she was discovered by the dogs and torn to pieces.

"Move," she mumbled. It was as if she were outside of her body, prodding it to action. "Get up."

Distantly, like a sleepwalker, she felt herself stand. Her eyes opened and she saw the road stretching before her in a moonlit blur. One foot stepped automatically forward, balancing her tottering weight - then the other - back and forth - more quickly now, until she was shuffling like a toddler taking her first shaky steps.

"Faster," she commanded.

Soon Sky found herself settling into a slow and painful jog, moving up the road away from Étoile.

By the time she reached the forest's edge, Sky was coming back into herself. Her chilled blood was coursing through her veins, and she had a clearer notion of what she was trying to do. It was too simple and desperate to be anything one might call a "plan," but Sky decided, above all else, she had to get home.

She followed the line of her own tracks in the snow where they came down out of the pines. She ran through the shadows, through that dreamy realm of owls and deer, trying to put distance between herself and the dogs.

But the dogs kept coming.

The snow grew deeper as Sky climbed the slope out of the valley. She slipped often, and the effort of picking herself up and starting off again and again soon began to take its toll. What little energy she had left was quickly running out.

"Come on, legs," she panted. "Go!"

But her wrenched and shivering body, no longer the dream it once was, could only endure so much abuse.

By the time she had risen above the tree line, the dogs were closing in.

Sky plunged through the deepening snow.

The mountains loomed in the distance, beckoning her forward, while the moon and stars watched from above.

Still, Sky pressed on, staggering, falling, picking herself up, and staggering forward once again. At one point she turned and gazed down the glacier. The dogs were there. She saw them loping and bounding along her trail.

"Oh," she said. They would be on her soon.

She looked to the side of the canyon. The cliffs appeared too far away to ever reach them before the dogs caught her, but it was her only chance. She turned from her path and floundered toward the nearest outcrop.

"Arrooooo!" howled the lead dog, signaling to the pack when he spied the girl in the snow. The other animals went mad with anticipation.

Sky didn't turn to see, but she sensed them there behind her - a writhing, steaming shadow glinting with fangs and burning eyes.

Ahead, at the top of a swell, stood a wall of granite too steep for dogs to climb. Sky thought, if I can only get there.

Her legs were nearly useless, but Sky willed them to carry her forward through that last barrier of soft snow. "Go," she said. "Go...Go...Go..." Each step carried her nearer to safety.

Now the dogs were so close she could hear their snapping jaws. She could almost feel their breath on the back of her neck. "Go..."

At last, she touched the stone. "Ah!" She had made it. But in the next instant, her hope melted away. Her hands were too cold. She couldn't feel the rock!

She pawed at the wall of granite, scratching for something to hold onto, but it was no good. Her hands were like stones. "Oh." They could not do what she asked.

Sky turned with her back to the wall, and then let herself slide down until she was sitting in the snow. Her head fell back. "Well," she sighed, giving herself up to complete weariness.

The dogs were right before her now, lunging wildly up the swell over the last few yards. Sky knew they were coming fast, but somehow they seemed to be moving so slowly, almost as if they were mired in thick moonlight. That gruesome moment she knew was coming seemed to be taking forever to arrive.

Sky thought of Gaston's green eyes; she thought of his candle. It made her sad, but it made her smile. She felt that tiny light flickering away in her own soul. It wavered and danced on its wick like a summer flower.

It was so small now in this enormous night.

Just a moment longer, Sky understood, and the flame would disappear.

"I would have liked to have seen the sea," she whispered.

And then everything went dark.

DREAM

IT WAS SUMMER.

Sky knew at once that it was.

She felt the sunshine on her eyelids; she smelled the delicate scent of wildflowers drifting over the heather.

"Mmm." She moaned with pleasure and stretched her arms and legs. She spread her fingers and toes and yawned a big, satisfying yawn. Never in her life had she felt so utterly comfortable. "Mmmmmm." Never had she felt so well rested.

Nearby, someone was laughing. "Oh, really," they said. "That's wonderful!" And then they laughed some more.

Someone else answered with something Sky could not quite hear. But she knew those voices. From somewhere. She did. Even if she couldn't quite place them.

"Who?" she asked, and opened her eyes.

A million stars blinked in the noonday blueness of the sky.

The translucent presence of the moon sailed over the friendly mountains.

Rising from her bed of flowers, Sky followed the voices to a little stream flowing out of some boulders into a blue pool. She climbed onto a tall rock and peered into the water. A white blur flashed in the depths, and then a long and elegant figure came to the surface. Sky recognized her in an instant.

"Mother!" she whispered.

The woman tread water in the pool. "Blue Sky." She smiled. "We're so glad you're here."

"Yes," came another voice. "Where on earth have you been?"

Sky turned to find her father and Nan and Old Stone lounging at the water's edge.

"We've all been wondering," said the doe, "when you would finally arrive."

Sky was so glad to see *everyone,* but she couldn't take her eyes from her father. He was just as she had always pictured him: he wore knickers and mountain boots and a red flannel shirt with the sleeves rolled up to his elbows. His face was deeply tanned from the glare of the glacier. Smile lines were etched at the corners of each of his golden brown eyes.

He stood and offered Sky his hand. "Here you go," he said. "Come rest with us for a while."

Sky grasped his fingers and stepped down. She knelt with the others on a patch of grass. Her mother then came from the pool and joined them, stretching herself to dry on a sun-washed boulder.

Sky was so pleased they were all together.

Everyone joked and laughed and told stories, and then the little group sat quietly, enjoying the song of the glacier.

Sky had never heard that music like she did now. Each note was as clear as a drop of water. She was especially surprised to find it held no sadness.

I must have been mistaken before, she told herself. I must have been hearing it wrong.

Her mother began to sing along with the glacier, and the two ethereal voices mingled and mixed until it was impossible to tell one from the other.

Sky listened, snuggled up close between her father and Nan and Stone. She felt a superb happiness.

But then her mother and the glacier stopped their song.

"Go on," urged Sky. "Please continue."

"No," said her mother. "It's time to stop for now."

"But why?"

Her mother smiled. "Because you have to go."

"Go? But I like it here."

"No," said Stone. "This isn't where you belong."

With a lump in her throat, Sky began to cry.

"Goodbye," said Nan.

"Goodbye," said Stone.

Then her father hugged her and kissed her on top of the head. "It's okay," he said. "Just be brave, and believe in yourself."

Sky nodded, wiping the tears from her face. She turned and, with everyone silently urging her on, she stepped into the pool.

"Oh!" she gasped.

The water was so much colder than she expected.

She turned once more to her family, but they were no longer there. And although she hated leaving this perfect place behind, Sky knew it was what she had to do.

"Okay," she said. "All right."

She stepped farther into the icy blue pool, its chill wrapping her in its embrace, and then, falling forward, Sky let herself sink and sink away like a stone.

CHAPTER FORTY-EIGHT

SHE WOKE WITH THE dawn.

In the stone room.

Beside the warm and bubbling pool.

Everything hurt, even her hair.

But she was pleased to find herself still in one piece; she was surprised to be alive.

She ran the tip of her tongue over her chapped and bleeding lips, and swallowed.

"Thank you," she whispered.

She was talking to her father and Old Stone.

"Thank you."

She thanked her mother and Nan for saving her from the dogs.

After a while, she carefully lifted herself from her bed and walked across the room. She laid her hand on her book, feeling its smooth cover beneath her raw fingertips, and then picked it up. She carried the book back to her place by the pool, and lay down once again.

A single cow sauntered through her imagination.

A camel sailed by in a boat.

Sky turned onto her side, the book hugged to her chest, a bemused and weary smile playing on her face.

Then she sighed.

She closed her tired blue eyes, letting herself drift away to a restful, dreamless sleep.

PART SEVEN

CHAPTER FORTY-NINE

BLUE SKY EMERGED ONCE more from the darkness and scrambled onto a tall boulder. She blinked her eyes at the brightness. She squeezed her fists, swaying in the sunny air.

She had eaten nothing for months except bits of lichen and moss, and she had grown eerily thin. Her knickers had holes in the knees, and her sweater hung on her gaunt frame like a rag. Her long black hair was patchy and tangled.

But none of that mattered to her now. It was finally spring. She had survived the winter.

Not as a dream.

And not as an ibex.

But as a girl.

Sky lifted her chin. "Just a girl."

She was eager to put those stormy nights behind her.

Stretching her arms above her head, she gazed up at the surrounding peaks. Melt-water streaked the cliffs. Gravel and ice rained onto the bergschrund. Sky needed to get up high. She felt the urgent desire for a wider view, but her old routes were off limits today. She would have to go the long way around.

Stiffly, she hopped onto a nearby boulder - and then the next - and then, carefully, the next, slowly working her way through the boulder field toward the open slope.

As her body limbered up, and as she remembered once again how to move in the mountains, Sky began to sense something stirring on the breeze, and in her thoughts. It had been a long time since she had felt that particular sensation, but she knew just what it was. The puzzle pieces of her life were coming together once again to form a plan. Of course, she didn't yet see what that plan might be, but she felt she soon would. She had learned to trust the stars, and to be patient. Through all of her adventures, she had learned to believe in herself.

Winded and sweating, she came onto the ridge.

To her surprise, she found three young ibex playing in the snow on the other side. The animals were so shocked to see a person that they froze in place, not knowing how to react.

"Hello," said Sky. "Are you having fun?"

The ibex glanced at one another, then back to Sky. Their horns were just beginning to sprout between their ears. Their fur was matted and wet from rolling in the snow.

Sky smiled. "Do any of you know Tuff and Brownie?"

The ibex cocked their heads and flicked their tails.

One little buck snorted, and bravely stomped the ground.

Another, a pretty doe, said, "Baaaaah!"

Then, as if on a signal, the three young beasts spun and raced away down the hillside.

"Well," whispered Sky. "Tell the boys hi for me when you see them."

She watched the animals bounding out of sight, the smallest twinge of sadness fluttering in her breast, the smallest fluttering of loss.

But then she continued up the ridge.

Once Sky gained the summit, she approached the stone woman quietly, without speaking. It felt wrong to wake her from her dream just now; it felt unnecessary. And anyway, Sky only wanted to be close with her for a while, the way a daughter might sit with her sleeping mother.

Sky dropped onto a flat rock, kneeling at the statue's feet. She scratched in the crust of snow, using her fingernails to dig for the plastic rose. But when she found it, she didn't pick it up. It appeared far too fragile. Some of the petals had separated from the stem, and the flower had become so faded it was nearly colorless. It looked like a collection of tiny, translucent bones.

Sky bent forward, sniffing the air above the broken rose. She might have been mistaken; she couldn't be sure, but Sky believed she could almost smell the faintest flowery fragrance, as if it were the lingering scent of a dream. She was about to bend closer, to sniff more deeply, when someone spoke behind her.

"Well, good day!"

Sky jumped to her feet.

"Oh, no!" said the man. "I beg your pardon."

Sky was too startled to speak.

There before her stood an alpinist. A rope was coiled over his shoulder, and he was breathing hard from his struggle in the thin air. He was old, his beard gray as granite.

"Forgive me," said the man, chuckling between breaths. He removed his stocking cap and bowed. "You appear..." He cleared his throat. "...as surprised to see me...as I am to see you."

"Yes," stammered Sky. "I'm... Well..." She tried to smile. "Hello."

The man wiped his brow with his sleeve, and pulled his cap back onto his head. "Hello. Hello." He limped a few steps closer, stooped beneath his backpack.

The man pinched his beard and studied Sky. "My goodness," he mumbled to himself.

Although she was somewhat embarrassed by her disheveled appearance, Sky was otherwise unafraid. She was quite certain this creature was an important piece of her puzzle, and she felt that *she* must surely be an important piece of *his* puzzle as well. He seemed so oddly familiar. Except that he was wearing clothes and had no horns, Sky might have mistaken him for Old Stone.

"My heavens!" said the man. "Where are my manners?" He wiped his hand on his shirt and held it out to Sky. "Marc Dujardin," he said. "At your service."

"Ah!" said Sky. (She sensed the stars watching down with amusement.)

She stared at the alpinist holding his hand in the air before her. Gaston hadn't mentioned that he was so old. She wasn't entirely sure what was proper, but Sky felt compelled to lift her own hand to his, letting her fingers touch his calloused palm.

"My name is Sky," she said. "Blue Sky."

The old man grinned, his golden eyes sparkling in the sunlight, and gently squeezed her hand. "A pleasure to meet you, my dear."

They stood motionless for a moment, just staring into one another's eyes, each appearing like an unexpected miracle to the other. Then they let go their hands.

"Well, Blue Sky." He swung his pack from his back.

"I'm about as peckish as a man can be after that climb. And you must be rather hungry yourself. So..." He reached into his pack. "May I offer you some lunch?"

Sky's stomach gurgled at the mention of food. "Sure," she said. "That would be nice."

And so the old man and the young girl had a picnic on the mountaintop. They watched over the canyon while eating bread and cheese.

"What a place!" said Master Dujardin. "This sunshine does my old bones a world of good."

Sky nodded politely, trying to chew slowly and not gulp her food. She could feel it making her stronger with every bite.

"You know," said the man, "I woke this morning, well before first light, remembering a dream I had when I was a boy. It came back to me just as vivid as it was all those years ago, as if it had been hiding all along, only waiting for this day to arrive." He shook his head thoughtfully. "Just waiting to bloom." He wiped the breadcrumbs from his whiskers. "If there's one thing I've learned, young lady - when your dreams whisper in your ear, you're best advised to pay attention."

The old man paused, his eyes shining, considering his words, and perhaps, Sky thought, reliving his secret boyhood dream. "We really have no choice when the mountains call." He bobbed his head and spread his arms wide to the massif. "And now, my dear Sky, I get to be here with you on this lovely day!" He laughed. "Wonderful!"

Sky swallowed a bite of cheese. "Hooray!" she said softly.

Still laughing, the old man pointed his sandwich at The Steeple. "And do you suppose anyone will ever climb that one all the way to the top?"

Sky looked at The Steeple, so sheer and gleaming like a castle in the sun. "Someday."

Master Dujardin nodded. "You're probably right. Some young enthusiast will come along, toting more energy than common sense, and find a way."

Sky thought of her father, and then of Gaston. She turned and squinted toward Étoile. It was already summer in the lower elevations; the valleys were green and the rivers were gushing with water running down from the mountains. Gaston had surely left weeks ago. In her mind, Sky could picture him walking away.

Master Dujardin offered her a drink from his canteen, and then gave her a piece of chocolate.

"Thank you," said Sky.

They sat side by side, sucking at the sweetness while watching the sun pass over the sparkling white glacier. Sky couldn't hear the glacier today. That wild lullaby was in a language she could no longer understand. But she remembered the happy-sad way it made one feel. And she knew she would always carry that inside of her, tucked away like a treasure.

The afternoon passed.

"Well," said the old man. He struggled to his feet, and arched his back. "As with all beautiful dreams, this one must end so the next might begin." He hobbled over to the stone woman, grasped her hand, and, peering into her placid face, winked. Then he turned and grabbed up his pack, twisting his arms into the straps.

Sky stood before him.

"You can be sure," he said, "if you ever visit Étoile, you have a place to stay if you need it. Just come by my shop."

Sky nodded. Everything was suddenly happening so fast.

Master Dujardin rested his hand on her shoulder,

and smiled once more. "Otherwise," he said, "no matter where you decide to be, good luck."

Sky knit her brow. All at once she felt so odd, as if part of her were made of stone, as if she were struggling to be completely awake. She needed something more from this old man, something other than chocolate and friendship, but she couldn't think what it might be. There was an important piece of her puzzle still missing from its place. A panic rose up inside of her as he prepared to leave.

The old alpinist hung his coiled rope over his shoulder and started down the ridge.

"Farewell, Blue Sky." He lifted his hand and waved as he moved away.

Sky stepped after him, but stopped.

She bit her lip.

Then she twirled on her heel and came back to her mother, leaning near. "What should I do?" she whispered.

The moon-white statue stood motionless before her.

Her eyes didn't blink.

Her stone lips didn't tremble.

Not one bit of her seemed to move in the least.

But Sky heard something. She did. Very faint, but

clear. One last time, like the final echo of a dream, the young girl was able to hear her mother's voice.

It came to her on the breeze, born from the deep blue sky.

Follow your dreams, whispered the statue. *Follow your heart.*

Sky spread her fingers over her chest. The rhythmic thump of her own heart bumped against her palm. Her panic melted away. She nodded once. Then she turned down the ridge to where the old man was working his way over the rocks and patchy snow.

"Excuse me!" she called. "Please wait!"

Master Dujardin stopped and gazed back curiously at Sky.

"I wonder," said Sky. "Could you..."

She was so excited she found it difficult to bring forth the right twist of words.

The old man waited.

"Could you please tell me," said Sky. She shrugged and held up her palms. "I wonder could you show me which way it is to the nearest sea."

Master Dujardin tipped his head and scratched his chin. Then he grinned. "Of course," he laughed. "Yes. By all means!" He squared himself to the sun, took his bearings, and then pointed into the distance. "Do you see that lowest place beyond the plains? There, where the sky comes down to kiss the earth?"

Sky searched the low horizon beyond the massif. "Yes! I see it!"

"Always keep the morning sun to your left. And follow the stars." He laughed one last time as he turned again to go. "I have no doubt, Blue Sky, that you'll surely find your way."

Sky stared at that far piece of the world, fixing it in her memory.

She leaned over and kissed the statue's cool stone cheek.

And then, with all the world at her feet, she set off to find the deep blue sea.

Look for the next title to be published by Brian Kindall:

Pearl

She is a girl made entirely of stone and she has been resting on the floor of the sea for a thousand years. At first glance, one might not think such an existence could be very exciting, but when a boy named Niko pulls her from the waves, Pearl's life seems only to have just begun. In a series of adventures that carries her to an exotic island grotto, a bloody revolution, a rat-infested tomb, and at last, to a peaceful mountain retreat, Pearl encounters crazed rebels, wise philosophers, and greedy grave robbers, as well as a few other friendly people and fish along the way. Through all of her perils, Pearl undergoes a magical transformation. What she will finally become depends upon her courage, her desires, and her faith in the very stars that seem to be guiding her to her final destiny.

38733286R00165

Made in the USA
Lexington, KY
26 January 2015